The Storm Magnet

KAREN I SAGE

CONTENTS

A PREDICTION

'What would you make of this news Vera?'

Lizzie lay on her bed talking to the poster on her wall. The young astronomer, Vera Rubin, was peering into a microscope at images of stars.

'Would you say, "We're still groping for the truth. This is in the realm of the unknown."?'

Lizzie knew Vera's interview on the MindPickings website by heart.

'Or would you say, "Astrology is the mad daughter to astronomy's wise mother. Don't believe a word of it"?'

I think another famous person said that. Not sure who.

If only her heroine could answer.

Lizzie was puzzling over her grandpa's words. A few hours earlier he'd prepared her astrological birth chart. It was a hobby of his. He wanted to do something special for her thirteen[th] birthday. Which was in two days' time! Yoo-hoo!

'How extraordinary!' he said. 'I've never seen anything like it.'

He slapped his forehead and his round, metal-rimmed spectacles jumped down his nose. Grandpa was excited. Lizzie could tell. His little, white moustache quivered like a nervous mouse.

'Jupiter is in a very strange position relative to Aries. It's in opposition to the moon. And there's an unusual Sun/Ceres combination. This can mean only one thing...[a thing. a] catastrophic natural event is heading this way and you are destined to stop it!'

Up to that point, Lizzie hadn't been listening. She was working through a tricky game on her handheld games console. Her avatar Pangloss was about to get squished if she didn't find the secret to...

'What did you say Grandpa?'

'Something big and bad's going to happen. You have to stop it, Lizzie!'

'Who ... me?'

'Don't believe a word of it!' Lizzie's mum shouted from the kitchen. The aroma of pea and ham soup and freshly baked bread drifted into the living room. She had reluctantly agreed to her father preparing Lizzie's birth chart and had been listening in on the conversation. She didn't want her dad filling Lizzie's head full of nonsense.

'The sequence of events starts on your birthday,' he said. 'You won't be alone. Just as well, because some sort of danger is indicated.'

'Don't scare her, dad!'

Lizzie pursed her lips and frowned.

'I'm not a child, Mum. I'll be a teenager soon. This could be the most interesting thing that's ever going to happen to me! You wouldn't mollycoddle me so much if I was a boy!'

'I'm just saying,' her mum sighed.

'There's one other thing,' Lizzie's grandpa said. 'A few numbers keep popping up on your chart. They must be important. Thirteen first, then eight, seven, and lastly five.'

How curious. Lizzie wondered what it all meant. After dinner, she'd gone upstairs to her bedroom. On the outside of the door she'd hung the sign:

THIS DOOR IS CLOSED FOR A REASON

That usually kept intruders away.

Surrounded by her favourite things, Lizzie could focus more easily. The gentle rotation of the planet ceiling mobile freed her mind. Inspiration came from her posters of Vera, marine explorer Sylvia Earle and astronaut Mae Jemison. If she was stuck on a problem, she'd flick through one of her treasured books. A shelf on the wall sagged under their weight. Among them, *The Fundamentals of Space Travel, A History of North America's First People, The World's Greatest Adventurers* and *Practical Skills in the Wilderness*. She considered these more reliable than the Internet as they were written by experts.

By the door on top of a chest of drawers she kept her prized holiday souvenirs. A piece of volcanic rock from Hawaii. Fossilised plant stems from British Columbia. A Beanie Baby bear dressed as a NASA astronaut. They'd gone to the space centre as a family the year before her dad died. Her mum said he'd bought her the bear. Lizzie scrunched up her eyes and tried to remember. It was no good. She knew her dad's face from photos, but she couldn't conjure up an image of him at that moment.

Lizzie eased herself off the bed and picked up the bear. *Who said I was too old to play with cuddly toys?* She threw it high in the air and caught it a few times. *Up to the stars! Up you go! And again! And again!*

'Now you've had your brain joggled Dr Sal, what do you think?'

She put her ear to its mouth.

'What's that you say? Speak up. I can't hear you. Why

don't I ask Josh? That's the best idea you've had in ages!'

***

Lizzie and Josh were science buddies at school. They shared a fascination in how the world worked, fuelled by their science teacher, Dr Galloway. Everyone called him Dr Galaxy because of his love of space. Weekly news bulletins from the International Space Station were his speciality.

'Astronauts from Russia, America and France are orbiting the earth four hundred kilometres above our heads,' he would say, 'in a structure the size of a six-bedroom house. They're planting lettuces up there right now!'

Dr Galloway's pairing of Lizzie and Josh had been inspired. Josh's measured approach to understanding the universe balanced out Lizzie's more impulsive nature. Whereas Lizzie tended to view things as black or white with a sprinkling of silver, a rainbow of explanations coloured Josh's reasoning.

Lizzie had fallen under Dr Galloway's spell when he talked about the importance of numbers in the world. She felt she'd glimpsed their magic when he told their class about the Golden Ratio. It was mind-boggling that the same number appeared throughout nature, in art and even in the iPod and the human face.

Her grandpa also loved numbers, but not the scientific kind. He believed in numerology, the cryptic relationship between numbers and events. He'd brought home a library book on the subject for Lizzie. She'd been reluctant to look through it at first. She wanted to be a scientist like Vera, Sylvia, Mae ... and Dad. Numerology was not science. But she loved her grandpa and didn't want to hurt his feelings. He was her co-conspirator after all. While her mum tried to keep her wrapped up in cotton wool like a fragile jewel, Grandpa encouraged her adventurous side. 'You're a rough diamond,' he said. 'You need to experience the world to smooth out those jagged edges so you can shine.'

Before meeting Josh, Lizzie decided to look up her birth chart numbers in the numerology book. *May as well see what it says. Grandpa will be pleased I've shown an interest.*

According to the book, thirteen was the number four (one add three) in numerology relating to a strong sense of responsibility. The number eight meant decisive and commanding. Five was her destiny number and seven related to her inner dreams. Mmm ... *I wonder if there's any truth in this strange pseudo-science?*

The following day during break she told Josh all she'd

learned.

'What do you think?' she said. 'How do you reckon these numbers might solve a looming disaster?'

'Well, I don't believe in birth charts and numerology. There is no scientific basis to them whatsoever. Then again, science can't explain everything in the universe. So ....'

'So ...?'

'So, assuming there is a grain of truth in all this number mumbo-jumbo, where do the numbers four, eight, five and seven appear together?'

'All over the place, especially in school! On the playground wall, in every classroom, in our exercise books - they're everywhere!'

Lizzie started pacing. *Think! Think!*

'Aargh! This is no good. How are we ever going to work it out?' she said.

'Cool it Lizzie. Let's stay focused and think this through. It's probably not as obvious as the actual figures themselves. They could refer to the number of something. You said a natural disaster is coming to the city? Maybe your numbers relate to something downtown.'

Downtown. What is there downtown? Buildings, roads, parks, cars, people, walkways … walkways …

Lizzie started to fizz with excitement.

'I've got it! I've got it! Where is that leaflet on the Skyway they handed out in school the other day?'

'Here it is,' said Josh, pulling one from his backpack.

'It's got to be the Skyway network around town!' said Lizzie. 'Thirteen is the number of feet the walkways are above street level. Three plus? one is four. There are fifty-nine bridges. Add the five and nine and you get fourteen; add the one and four to make five. Sixteen kilometres of walkway. One plus six is seven. It was opened in 1970, which is the number eight in numerology. It's too much of a coincidence not to be important.'

'Hang on a minute,' said Josh. 'What's all this adding of numbers about?'

'Never mind. Trust me,' said Lizzie. 'I know I'm right. What do you think?'

'Well, it's certainly a theory of sorts. But what do you hope to find in the Skyway?'

'The answer to how I'm going to save the city, of course!'

THE WHITE-HAIRED STRANGER

BEEP! BEEP! BEEP! BEEP! BEEP! BEEP!

Lizzie rolled over and peered at the digital display. Seven o'clock. *Uurgh!* She threw the Luke Skywalker training orb at the wall. It bounced back, bonking her on the head. Ow! A restless night had left her feeling jaded. Now she felt annoyed as well. It took her a while to register what day it was. *Saturday 26th November. That's... That's... My birthday! Yay! If Grandpa's correct, something big will be set in motion today. Nothing will ever be the same again. Maybe I'll become a Jedi and save the galaxy!*

She rubbed her head and climbed out of bed, kicking the silenced alarm clock across the floor. *Now I must battle my way to Devaron.* Lizzie moved forward, swiping the air with an imaginary light sabre until she reached the bathroom. *At last! I see the temple.* She returned the weapon to its scabbard and entered.

***

Lizzie had persuaded Josh to explore the Skyway with her. He hadn't seemed keen.

'I'm not sure. I really wanted to build this solar powered robot Glen gave me in exchange for my Minator video game,' he said.

'Come on Josh. I become a teenager tomorrow. How can you refuse your best science buddy's wish on her birthday?' she said. 'Besides I need your superior problem-solving brainpower on a mission like this.'

That should do it. Flatter his ego and he'll agree to anything.

'Oh, alright then. I don't think we're going to find anything earth-shattering but there's no harm in looking.'

'Don't tell Mum,' said Lizzie. 'She worries too much and will be happier thinking we're going to the Science Museum.'

Lizzie's mum had warned her off wandering inside the Skyway, even in a twosome. Its maze of tunnels, walkways and bridges connected most of the tall office blocks in the city, but also hosted many of the seedier activities in town.

Lizzie had been agitating to go ever since breakfast. As

soon as she saw Josh approaching their house, she grabbed her coat.

'Bye Mum!'

'Bye sweetie! Make sure you're home for dinner. There's a special surprise waiting for you! And stick together, you two!'

'We will.'

***

Lizzie and Josh lived a few streets away from each other in a suburb of Macimanito. The name meant 'demon' in the language of the First People who'd lived there. According to legend an evil spirit lay sleeping under the streets. When certain planets moved into celestial alignment, the beast would wake up and wreak havoc on the population. Centuries ago, there had been cases of mass hysteria when the entire population had been transfixed by flashing lights and strange shapes in the sky.

Lizzie didn't believe the story. She was a scientist and was convinced that all the recorded incidents had been natural phenomena not uncommon in that part of the world. A mythical creature? What utter nonsense. The First People had lots of stories handed down from generation to generation but that didn't make them true, did it?

At least there's no sign of a malevolent force awakening this morning. Not yet, anyway. Where is everyone?

The whole city seemed to be fast asleep, there were so few people about. The emerging light cast an eerie yellowish glow in the sky. It lit up a band of cloud circling the city below, like a halo of tarnished bronze.

The two friends walked to the Z-train station a few blocks from Lizzie's home. She took comfort from the familiarity of the rows of identical wooden houses in varying shades of grey and brown. Each had a veranda out front, a steeply sloping roof and two round windows on the first floor. They looked like a line of benevolent giants watching them as they passed by.

Echoing the quietness of the streets, Lizzie and Josh strolled side by side in companionable silence, lost in their own thoughts. Lizzie's were an excited jumble of possible routes through the Skyway. Josh was wondering why he'd agreed to come along at all. They were probably wasting their time.

As they rounded a corner, the red tiled roof of the Z-train station came into view. Lizzie felt a memory spark, too fleeting to capture. The moment unnerved her, and she shivered.

They crossed the road and went up the ramp on to the

deserted station platform. Lizzie stood with shoulders hunched, her hands stuffed into the pockets of her thick, quilted winter coat. Her frizzy black hair poked out from the hood, which framed her heart-shaped face in its furry trim. Behind square, black-rimmed spectacles, intense, quizzical dark brown eyes stared into the middle distance. Every now and then she stomped her feet in their thick-soled, knee-high padded boots to keep her feet warm.

Josh, a few inches taller than Lizzie, adopted a more relaxed pose as he scrutinised the map of the train network on the platform notice board. Every now and then he ruffled his messy light-brown mop of hair.

'Let's enter the Skyway at the library,' said Lizzie, as Josh came and stood beside her, 'and work our way eastwards. Remember to keep an eye out for those numbers. They must be significant.'

Lizzie was convinced the numbers hadn't served their sole purpose in leading her to the Skyway. Why would they appear in her birth chart, only to result in a dead-end? She had to find out how the Skyway *was* related to Grandpa's prediction. If she was successful, no, *when* she was successful in saving the city, her dad would be so proud of her. She knew there was no scientific evidence for life after death, but secretly she hoped her dad was watching her from somewhere up in the stars.

'What happens if we find nothing but corridors leading to offices, food outlets and exit signs?' said Josh.

'Oh, we will I can feel it in my bones.'

Taking their cue from Lizzie's words, the reverberations of an approaching train sent a sonic rumble through the concrete platform and up through the soles of their feet. A squeal of brakes, the grinding sound of metal on metal and the train came to a halt in front of them. Its entire length was sheathed in a printed scaly skin of bilious green, giving it to the look of a gigantic serpent.

Lizzie pushed the yellow flashing button. The doors opened with a clunk. Stepping inside they looked around. There was only one other person in the carriage: A huge man dressed in a long tweed overcoat, dark brown trousers and trainers. He sat at one end of the compartment, hands thrust into pockets, his tawny face obscured by long, straight, white hair.

Josh and Lizzie sat together as far away from him as possible.

'Once we're in the Skyway we must focus on the numbers,' whispered Lizzie.

The train started to snake its way through the suburbs towards the city centre, which lay in a bowl-shaped valley. Every few minutes a recorded message came over the loudspeakers announcing the next stop.

Halfway into their journey a deep, guttural voice emerged from the veil of hair.

'It'll do you no good. Poking around up there.'

'Are you talking to us?' said Josh.

'Well who else would I be talking to?' said the man.

Josh felt foolish and slumped forward in his seat.

'What do you mean poking around up there? Poking around up where?' said Lizzie.

She thought the man was rude, but she couldn't help being curious.

'I know where you're going, young lady. I'm simply warning you it's been attempted before and no good came of it.'

What an annoying man! Who does he think he is?

'It's none of your business where we're going or what we're doing,' she said.

So there!

'Just stay away, that's all I'm saying. You'll regret it if you don't.'

As the train stopped, the man sprang up from his seat, pushed the button and exited the carriage.

Lizzie was puzzled by the encounter. What did this stranger know about the Skyway? Why was he warning them off? She remembered putting her grandpa's comment about danger to the back of her mind. She'd been so excited. Now it resurfaced and she wondered what it meant.

What would Mum think if anything happened to me?

She'd asked Josh to come along because she knew her mum wouldn't let her go anywhere in the city alone, but was it fair to put him in danger too?

'He was a bit of an odd ball,' said Josh. He was still smarting from the man making him look silly.

'Probably just trying to scare us. He did look rather strange. Did you notice how he kept his face and hands hidden?'

'Yeah. Kind of creepy.'

CENTRE STREET NORTH EAST

'This is our stop,' said Lizzie. 'Come on, time to explore!'

THE CONTROL POD

Kitchi fled from the Z-Train before the interlopers could ask more questions. It had been a risky strategy, allowing himself to be seen with them, but he had to warn the youngsters. Others had tried to unlock the secret of the Skyway and all had met a grisly end.

He sprinted into a gleaming metal stairwell that led to the elevated walkway. Taking three steps at a time with his long, loping legs, he soon reached the top. A straight, arched corridor stretched out in front of him. Its glossy, red-tiled floor disappeared into the distance like a river of blood. Black and white interlocking birds decorated the walls. Every few hundred yards the pattern was broken by a metal-framed glass door. Each door opened out into the cathedral-like central lobby of an office building. Inside, towering potted plants stretched skyward to the floors above. Between buildings the corridor transformed into a transparent metal cage of silver and glass that looked out over the streets below.

Running across the first bridge, Kitchi didn't notice the shambling figure on the pavement below. Dressed in a mishmash of clothes, the man pushed a shopping trolley spilling over with stuffed plastic bags. A grin spread across the watcher's bearded face. He recognised those distinctive white locks, luminous against the darkening sky. Our friend is on the move again, he thought, pulling up the collar of his moth-eaten coat.

Kitchi ran along the passageway until the yellow ribbon of another corridor intersected his path and a circular landing area marked a crossway. Swiftly looking around, he darted across to the wall opposite, placed one hand on the wall, and with the fingers of the other danced out a code on a touchpad hidden behind a fire alarm box. The panel moved sideways on silent runners, allowing access and then slid back into place. Leaning with his back against the door, Kitchi waited for his breathing to return to normal before entering the elevator. Thirty seconds later and forty storeys higher, he stepped out into The Control Pod.

'Ah! You're back!' The voice of Reggie Grant boomed out across the room. He stood leaning forward, his arms straight, the knuckles of both hands pressed into the desk in front of him. His eyes scanned a bank of monitors mounted high up on the wall. Wearing immaculate beige overalls with electrician's pouch, rubber-soled boots and high voltage gloves, Reggie looked every inch the chief engineer. His lean frame, tidy features and steel-rimmed glasses suggested a man with an eye for detail and order. A group of fifteen technicians sat in front of computer terminals arranged in a half moon shape behind him.

'Any luck, old chap?' Reggie asked, not turning his attention away from the monitors.

'My instinct was right,' replied Kitchi. 'There's something special about this girl.'

'But isn't that what you said about those three young hackers and that nice middle-aged couple? You know what happened to them. I don't want this to end just as .... messily.'

'This girl's different. She's the daughter of Charles Chambers, one of the geophysicists I worked with on the Skyway project. On her mother's side her heritage is Takoda, a First People's tribe. I've been following her progress since she was a baby. Today is her thirteenth birthday. She's been gifted the key.'

'How can you be so sure?'

'I overheard her talking to her friend. She spoke of numbers. She's a smart kid. Maybe she's worked out the real purpose of the Skyway. In which case, there's every chance her numbers, wherever they come from, are the code we've been searching for.'

'But you warned them off?'

'Of course I did, but that won't stop her. She's keen, very keen, and a spirited little thing. I don't see her giving up until she's figured out exactly what's happening and where her numbers fit in. We need to tread carefully and not frighten her off. And we mustn't let Gildchrist get to her first or that woman will use the code to destroy the city and to satisfy her own greed.'

'Let's hope you're right this time. How long have we been trying to crack this thing?'

'Nine years.'

'Nine long years trying to find the correct number sequence, and waiting for a thunderstorm to test each one. Despite the wonders of technology, we still haven't found the code. There are too many possible combinations and too few opportunities to try them out. Unless we hit on the right code soon, the city is finished. I'll never understand why Lancing didn't write down the numbers instead of just telling his most trusted engineers. One lightning strike and poof! That was the end of them all, some of the greatest engineering brains of their day and the code to maximise the Skyway's power.'

An ominous rumble shook the Control Pod. A bundle of black fur with one ear missing leapt up from a nearby chair on to Reggie's chest. It let out a startled 'meow!'

'It's alright, Celeste,' soothed Reggie. He gently pulled the cat off and popped her inside his overalls to muffle both the sight and sound of the onslaught to come.

'Safety gear gentlemen! You too, Kitchi,' said Reggie. He glanced up at the curved window encircling the room a hundred and ninety metres above street level.

In the sky outside, fat lobes of mammatus clouds hung like bulbous polyps on the underside of a blue-grey mass which rolled across the top of the skyscrapers. It enveloped the control tower like the smothering arms of a gargantuan monster. Bruised and angry, it spat out shards of fiery fury.

An explosion of brilliant white light filled the room as the lightning struck the tower. It followed the path of least resistance through the metal frame of the Skyway and into the earth.

A series of red warning lights started flashing on first one, and then all the screens on the walls.

'Stand by to energise the pods!' shouted Reggie. 'We knew this was coming, so you should all be ready with the latest activation sequence. Macimanito, you devil! You're not going to get us this time!'

A SECRET PASSAGE

Lizzie and Josh stepped off the train and looked around. To their left, two people huddled together on a bench in a three-sided glass shelter. It was designed to take the edge off the icy breeze whistling down the platform. Further along, a figure in a long, black coat and hat stood leaning against a ticket machine, staring ahead of him.

'Let's get out of the cold,' said Lizzie. 'Look at the sky – a storm's brewing.'

They quickly walked along the sloping platform and on to the pavement. The central library was two blocks away. Lizzie sensed the city stirring into life - the grating metallic sound of shop window shutters being raised, the purr of delivery van engines, the shrill whistle of a freight train rumbling along in the distance. People on their way to work scurried between buildings, clutching take-away coffees in mittened hands. The occasional plume of steam puffed out from the side of a wall.

So far, so normal.

On the corner of 20th Street NE and Centre Avenue, Lizzie and Josh entered the library. As the heat hit them, they unzipped their coats, pocketed their gloves and took the stairs up to the first floor. Here, one side of the building opened out on to an elevated bridge. This took them across the road to the entrance of the Skyway network.

'Right - which way shall we go?' said Josh.

Silence.

'You do have a plan, don't you?'

'Who needs a plan? This is a journey into the unknown.'

'Fine.' He strode off along one of the four radiating walkways.

'Hang on a minute.'

'I thought you said you didn't have a plan.'

'Will you stop and give me a moment?' said Lizzie.

What's wrong with him? Probably wants to get back to his stupid robot.

Lizzie furrowed her brow and moved her nose up and down. She looked like an annoyed rabbit sniffing the air. It was a look Josh knew well from science class: She was thinking.

'Well?'

Lizzie raised her hand to her throat. On a black leather thong hung the talisman her grandpa had given her that morning for her birthday. She felt the smooth surface of the bone arrowhead. 'This was your great-grandfather's - keep it safe,' he'd whispered, pressing it into her palm so her mother wouldn't see.

'I think we should take the blue path towards the west,' she said.

'Really? Why's that, Mystic Meg?'

'Mmm … gut feeling.'

'Right. So first you start believing in ridiculous astrological predictions, then numerology nonsense and now airy-fairy hunches.'

'I don't believe in them.'

'Looks that way to me. You can't be a scientist if you believe in all that stuff,' said Josh.

'Oh yeah? Watch me!'

Lizzie stormed off.

'Wait. Wait!'

Josh caught up with her.

'What is it now?' she said.

'You're going the wrong way.'

'What?'

'You said the blue walkway.'

Smarty pants!

She turned around and started along a different route.

As they walked along the corridor, the overhead strip light flickered. The intertwining snakes painted on the curved walls seemed to writhe and squirm. Lizzie had the unsettling feeling she was being funnelled into an ever-decreasing space. There were no doors leading off this section and no-one passed them in either direction.

Up ahead, they saw a glass cabinet on top of a podium. It threw out a welcoming glow. As they reached it, Josh peered inside the cube.

'Looks like some sort of art installation.'

Four translucent glass sea creatures were suspended inside the cabinet on thin wires. A smoky grey, lozenge-shaped sea urchin. An aquamarine jellyfish with luminous tendrils. A dark orange squid with bulbous eyes. A lilac box fish with open mouth. Lizzie's anger evaporated at the sight of them.

'They're gorgeous,' she said, transfixed.

Why have I never noticed these before?

She raised her hand to touch the side of the cabinet. As she pressed her palm against the glass, it went straight through. Surprised, she withdrew it sharply. How peculiar!

Tentatively, she tried again. Sure enough, it was as if the sides of the cabinet didn't exist.

What just happened? It doesn't make sense.

'It must be some sort of hologram,' said Josh.

'You try it,' said Lizzie.

Josh slowly moved his hand towards the glass. His palm contacted the cool surface.

'No, it doesn't work for me. Try again.'

Lizzie pushed her hand through, fingers first this time. She gently touched the glass creatures one at a time, careful not to dislodge them. Each carried a line of nodules on its back. She stroked them in turn a few times. *Hold on!* She turned to Josh, her mouth wide open. She was on the point of saying something when they heard a loud clunk, followed by a whooshing sound. A doorway opened in the wall next to the cabinet.

They looked at each other, their eyes wide with astonishment.

'It's a secret passage,' said Josh. 'What did you do?'

'I'm not sure. Quick, let's get inside before the door closes.'

Lizzie stepped into the entrance. Josh hesitated.

'Come on,' she said.

'But what happens if we can't get back?'

'Just get in! Where's your sense of adventure?'

Josh grimaced. He remembered Lizzie's mum's last words to them, 'stick together you two', and quickly joined her on the other side of the door. Instantly, it closed behind them.

***

The watcher saw them disappear into the wall. He'd followed them from the Z-train station. He walked up to the glass cabinet and pushed against it. Nothing happened. He leaned hard against the panel behind. No luck there either.

'Drat!' That girl's trouble and I've lost her, he thought, before heading back towards the Gildchrist building.

27

DR HAROLD LANCING

The instant the door closed behind them, Lizzie and Josh were plunged into a darkness so complete they couldn't see their hands in front of their faces.

'Are you OK Josh?'

Lizzie knew her friend was terrified of the dark. In science class one day, Dr Galloway had wanted to demonstrate how certain chemicals luminesce. He had taken them in groups into the dark room. Josh had been fine until the lights were switched off, when he'd started hammering on the door to be let out. Lizzie had been shocked by her friend's phobia. She'd realised not everyone was as fearless as her. *Not very sympathetic? Phobias could be better understood/portrayed?*

She felt for Josh's arm with one hand and gave it a reassuring squeeze; with the other, she fumbled for a torch in the large inside pocket of her coat. It was full of things she'd decided might come in useful. Feeling around with her fingertips, she touched the cold metal barrel of the torch, pulled it out and switched it on.

'There!' she said.

The passageway lit up in the beam of the flashlight. Josh visibly relaxed; His rigid shoulders dropped slightly, his frozen stare thawed.

'Phew, that was close,' he said. 'I thought I was going to be sick.'

Lizzie explored the space with her torch. Shadows danced off the smooth, grey walls of the narrow, downward curving passage.

'Look,' she said, pointing the beam at something on the wall. 'It's a framed newspaper cutting ... from 3rd October 1970.' She wiped her sleeve across the surface of the glass so she could see more clearly behind the film of dust.

'Listen to this.' She started to read:

"Mayor opens Lancing's Skyway

Today's Alfred Klein, Mayor of Macimanito, ~~today~~ officially opened the Skyway, an elevated walkway connecting major office and municipal buildings in the city. This new development, designed by the award-winning architect and scientist Dr Harold Lancing, will provide a warm, safe route around the city in the harsh winter months. It signals the completion of Macimanito's regeneration as a city fit for the 20th century.

The ribbon-cutting ceremony took place at 3pm at the Town Hall entrance to the Skyway. In attendance were local government officials and dignitaries, Dr Lancing and his team, and invited members of the local community.

The Skyway network 13ft above street level comprises 16km of walkway, including 59 enclosed bridges. The walkways are colour-coded for ease of navigation. A First People's group of artists was commissioned to create the murals throughout the Skyway, which depict flora and fauna native to North America.

Stairwells at street level and inside office buildings clearly signposted 'Skyway' provide access to the elevated walkway, which was built using state-of-the-art materials at a cost of $200m."

'There's a photograph as well,' said Lizzie, 'with a caption. It says, "*Pictured above are (left to right) Chief Engineers George Sykes and Richard Hartmann, Dr Harold Lancing, Mayor Klein, Council Leader Donald Cameron and Community Leaders*

Ethel King and Stanley Murdoch."

Lizzie and Josh craned their necks forward to look at the photo more closely. Dr Lancing and Mayor Klein stood in the middle of the group. They were shaking hands and looking at the camera. The other participants stood either side of them with their hands clasped in front of them. Everyone looked very pleased with themselves.

Lizzie shone the torch further along the wall.

'There are more newspaper cuttings. Look!'

A series of framed news stories traced the progress of the Skyway, from the announcement that the Council had selected Dr Harold Lancing for the job, through the various construction milestones to its completion and final opening.

'It says here,' said Josh, reading the framed cutting nearest the far end of the passageway, 'that *"Dr Lancing is a specialist in 'structures with positive conductive attributes',"* whatever that means, *"particularly bridges and tower blocks, for which he has won several awards in Europe and the Far East."'*

'I wonder what he's doing now,' said Lizzie. She was only half-listening as she tried pulling a long, vertical steel handle attached to a door at the end of the passage.

Josh, remembering how the wall of the Skyway had opened, said, 'Try pushing it sideways.'

Lizzie did as he suggested. The door slid open with a

pneumatic hiss. They stood for a moment looking at the scene in front of them.

The square room had windows on two sides. Blinds hid the view. Dark wood panelling covered the bottom third of the two other walls. Ornate plasterwork adorned the coving and a central ceiling rose, from which dangled an old-fashioned glass lampshade in the shape of an inverted tulip. Above the panelling every inch of space was pinned with undecipherable engineering drawings on huge sheets of paper. Three wooden office desks and chairs, positioned against the walls, faced into the room. Their surfaces were littered with books and papers, pencils and drawing instruments. In the centre of the room on a raised podium was a scale model of the Skyway, encased in glass. A thick carpet of dust covered everything.

'Wow!' said Josh.

'Looks like some sort of office.'

Stepping into the room, Lizzie noticed bits of machinery on oil-stained newspapers in one corner. Against an inner wall a stack of notebooks leaned precariously. At the foot of an old-fashioned coat stand by the door stood a pair of brown, lace-up shoes.

She walked round to take a closer look at one of the desks. 'Hey, there's a coffee cup here with ... yuck!' she said, peering inside. 'It looks like mold has hardened in the bottom and there's something sticky on the handle.'

'Same here,' said Josh. He'd sat behind one of the other desks and put his feet up. 'And a half-finished letter from.... Dr Harold Lancing! Hey, this must be *his* office!'

'But where are we exactly?' said Lizzie. She gently pulled up one of the window blinds to try and find her bearings. A shower of dust motes flew into the air. Outside, the sky had darkened and an explosion of light burst from the top of the communications tower in the centre of town. There followed the low rumble of thunder.

'I think we're in one of the older buildings that must have survived Dr Lancing's remodelling of the city,' she said, answering her own question. 'But there's only one way into and out of this room - through a hidden corridor off the Skyway. Why would Dr Lancing and his engineers need to be so secretive about the work they were doing for the City Council? I thought everyone knew about his work. It just doesn't add up!'

'They seem to have left in an almighty hurry,' said Josh looking around. Lizzie followed his gaze. Upturned rubbish bins, jackets on the backs of chairs and pencils carelessly thrown down on unfinished drawings suggested a hasty departure.

'Looks like it's been unoccupied for years. There's dust everywhere. I wonder if we're the first people to set foot in it since it was abandoned.'

How did *we manage to get in?*

Their entrance had been so peculiar. She couldn't quite figure it out.

It's as if the office found us rather than the other way around.

Lizzie dismissed the thought. She mustn't let herself slip into the realms of the unexplained. The only magic she believed in was the magic of numbers. They could explain just about anything. A niggling uncertainty, however, had wormed its way into her mind.

'I wonder what happened?' she said.

'Well, this could have something to do with it,' said Josh. He held up the letter he'd been reading. 'It's from Dr Lancing to someone called Klaus Schilling at a company in Berlin called Comwerk. It's dated 15th June 2011. It says, "Dear Klaus, further to our telephone conversation this morning, this is to confirm that we are in urgent need of ten new transponders for our pods. This is vital to ensure timely communications across the Skyway, which, as you are aware, is an exemplar in its field. We have already suffered one incident and without fully functioning transponders ...." It ends there. He didn't have time to finish the letter.'

'Pods? Transponders?'

'I've no idea what a pod is but I know about

transponders. There was a news story on television about a mobile phone network not working properly because the communications satellite transponders were malfunctioning. My dad told me a transponder is a device that can receive and transmit radio signals,' said Josh.

Lizzie had stopped listening when Josh was halfway through his explanation. She'd been distracted by the Skyway model in the middle of the room. Her eyes followed the route of the miniature walkway round the scale-model of the city.

'Do you realise,' she said, 'that the Skyway is in the shape of a pentagram.'

'A penta ... what?'

'A pentagram. A five-pointed star,' said Lizzie.

'And?'

'And ... a pentagram is like a geometric version of the Golden Ratio.'

'The golden what?'

'Keep up, Josh, keep up. Don't you remember Dr Galloway telling us all about the Golden Ratio and how it appears all over the place - in flowers, in trees, everywhere. It signifies the optimum natural order of things in the world. The attractiveness of someone's face, for example, can be measured by how closely the distances between the eyes, nose and mouth fit the Golden Ratio.'

'Ooo! How does mine measure up,' said Josh. He pouted his lips and turned his head to one side.

'Oh, be serious! Do you know what this means?'

'No, but I'm sure you're going to tell me.'

'This means that Dr Lancing deliberately remodelled the city based around the Golden Ratio. But why? Maybe the Skyway isn't simply an elevated walkway around town.'

'You've lost me now,' said Josh.

'Well, I know someone who might be able to help us,' said Lizzie, heading for the door.

'Come on. Let's go!'

TONI GILDCHRIST

Toni Gildchrist sat with her back turned to a huge glass and steel desk. She was dressed in a dove grey pants suit *pantsuit? (ou wod)* shot through with gold threads. A crisp white shirt, diamond stud earrings and polished black lace-up shoes completed the ensemble. Her chin rested on one hand, a pensive look on her tanned face.

She gazed at the low-lying sun. Suspended between two city skyscrapers it looked like the bloodied eye of an angry god. It radiated its energy through the floor-to-ceiling windows in front of her, reflecting off her silvery hair. Shimmering shards of light danced around her head. She wondered what was so important that her assistant had called her into the office on a Saturday.

There was a knock at the door and Clarissa's

immaculate five-foot-two-inch frame appeared.

'They're here, Madam. Shall I show them in?'

Gildchrist spun round and nodded her head.

Two men entered the room. One was tall and lanky with a swarthy complexion, scruffy beard and clothes to match. The other, dressed casually in jeans, jacket and trainers was clean-shaven with short, mousy brown hair.

'Well come in, come in,' Gildchrist said impatiently. 'Stand there.' She pointed to a spot in front of her desk.

'This better be good. I don't care for being dragged away from my weekend pursuits for some trivial bit of gossip.'

'Oh, this isn't trivial,' the two men said in unison.

'Kitchi ....' they both started to say. 'You first,' said one. 'No, you first,' said the other.

'For pity's sake, get on with it!' roared Gildchrist.

One watcher put his palm on his chest and nodded at the other to indicate he was going to speak first.

'Kitchi is up to something,' he said. 'I saw him legging it along the Skyway from the direction of the Z-train stop.'

'He's contacted a girl called Lizzie Chambers and her companion Josh Stapleton,' said the other watcher. 'I followed them into the Skyway and saw them disappear through a hidden door in the blue sector. She seemed to know the code to gain access.'

'The blue sector?' said Gildchrist. 'Are you sure? Whereabouts?'

'Right next to the glass sea aquarium sculpture commissioned by Dr Lancing.'

'Now that is interesting,' muttered Gildchrist to herself.

'Good work, men. Keep watching both Kitchi and the girl. You know where they stay?'

'Yes Sir, I mean Madam,' both watchers said together.

'Find out as much as you can about the girl and her companion,' she said. 'Off you go then!' She dismissed them with a wave of her hand when they showed no sign of budging.

The two men left the way they had come. Smiles crept on to their faces. Former partners in the police force, they'd relished the opportunity of working for one of the city's big names in mining. Toni Gildchrist had taken them on as 'her eyes and ears' and paid them three times their former salary. 'I want you to be invisible,' she'd said to them. 'You are watchers - nothing more, nothing less. Don't try anything clever; it will only end in tears, and they won't be mine.'

'D'you reckon this is the one then?' asked the shorter one of the two in a thin, reedy voice.

'Could be,' replied the other.

'Let's hope so for their sakes,' said the smaller man

chuckling. 'Wouldn't want to see her and her little friend fried like the others.'

'No indeed,' replied his companion. 'The smell was awful!' He wafted his hand in front of his face.

They exited the building and went their separate ways.

***

Deep in thought, Gildchrist stood looking out of her office window at the cityscape. The sunlight bounced between the glistening glass surfaces of the tall office blocks. Each reflected the image of its nearest neighbour.

Ah, so pretty at this time of the day, Gildchrist thought to herself. But not for long. If this girl holds the key to the Skyway and I can make it mine, Kitchi and his merry men will fail in their attempts to sequence the pods correctly and boom! It's only a matter of time before Macimanito's monster moves the heavens to destroy the city and I'll be able to harvest the riches that lie beneath.

She turned and looked at a faded photograph hanging on the wall next to the door. Four men wearing broad-brimmed hats, braces and boots ~~covered in dirt~~ dirt carved, stared back at her. Gildchrist searched the face of her great-grandfather in the centre of the picture. He had been one of the ordinary men who'd travelled north to prospect for gold in the Yukon territory during the gold rush of 1896. 'I'm going to make you proud,' she said aloud to herself. Like her great-grandfather and grandfather before her, she too would make her fortune from mining the earth's treasures. *If only Papa were here to see me achieve my heart's desire.* A gambler with little business sense, he had squandered the family's riches, leaving Gildchrist and her mother penniless before abandoning them. Gildchrist remembered the humiliation of being moved from a fee-paying school to the local state school. Her classmates had taunted her for being the fatherless rich kid. Despite this, she'd continued to love him. She wanted nothing more than to prove she could rebuild the family's fortunes and make the Gildchrist name synonymous with wealth and power once more.

A spear of light caught the edge of a huge solitaire diamond on the little finger of Gildchrist's left hand, throwing off a kaleidoscope of twinkling fragments. She smiled inwardly.

'There are plenty more where you came from,' she said, kissing the gleaming gem.

GRANDPA REMEMBERS

An other-worldly melody filled the living room. Lizzie's grandpa sat in the paisley-patterned armchair with his slippered feet resting on a matching foot stool. His head had fallen forward, eyes closed.

Lizzie's first instinct on rushing into the room was to wake him from his reverie. She was so excited about finding Dr Lancing's office she couldn't wait to tell him. But something stopped her. She saw him, for the first time, as the elderly gentleman he was.

He looks so old. So tired. When did this happen?

She felt her world shift slightly on its axis. As a child, she had assumed, she had hoped, that his energy would never fade, that somehow, he would live forever. Now it dawned on her that he wouldn't always be there for her.

Her beloved Grandpa, her mentor and confidant. She watched as his mouth formed into a gentle smile and his eyes danced behind their eyelids.

I think I know who he's dreaming about. Alawa, my grandma.

Lizzie's grandfather often talked about his darling wife and how they'd met. She'd been a beauty with long, black shiny hair reaching all the way down her back. Her eyes were dark, her skin honey-coloured, her cheekbones high and proud. When she had started at his high school, he had been instantly drawn to her. She was of mixed heritage, her father one of the First People, a full-blooded and ferocious-looking warrior, her mother a pretty, curly-haired redhead of Irish ancestry. As a result, her classmates teased her relentlessly, calling her all sorts of names. Alawa maintained a dignified silence, but George McLeod knew she was hurting inside and sprang to her defence if anyone mocked her in his presence. A friendship blossomed between the two youngsters which grew into a romantic attachment and eventually marriage.

Lizzie's mum had been their only child and Alawa had lived long enough to see Lizzie enter the world but no longer more. As one life ended, another began. As the years passed, the void left by Alawa's death had gradually been filled by the spirited, energetic Lizzie. She and her grandpa had become closer when he moved in with them after

Lizzie's dad Charles, a geophysicist, disappeared, presumed dead, on an assignment in Africa when Lizzie was only six years old.

'Ah, Lizzie!' said her grandpa, shaking slightly as he woke up. 'How was your day?'

'Well, you know I said me and Josh were going to the Science Museum?'

'Mmm ....'

'Well we didn't go there. We went to explore the Skyway instead, but you mustn't tell Mum.'

'I thought as much. I knew you were up to something. You had a twinkle in your eye. Why do you think I gave you that arrowhead that belonged to your great granddad? He was from the Takoda tribe. They believed animals had supernatural powers. That necklace is made of buffalo bone. It kept your great-granddad safe all his life, or so he believed.'

'We found something, Grandpa. In the Skyway, or at least just off the Skyway.'

'And what might that be?'

'The office of Dr Lancing.'

'Dr Harold Lancing? Are you sure?'

'There were all these newspaper cuttings about him, and pictures and books and papers everywhere and drawings on the walls and piles of note-books and bits of machinery and coffee cups and a model of the Skyway and even a pair of shoes!' Lizzie's words came out in a flood of excitement, her hands gesticulating wildly as she explained what they'd discovered.

'Slow down, slow down girl-and keep your voice low. Your mother's in the back room preparing your birthday dinner ... whoops! It was meant to be a surprise!'

'Never mind that, Grandpa. Who exactly is Dr Lancing?'

'Well,' he said, rubbing his chin thoughtfully. 'Where shall I begin?'

'When I was a very young man, before me and your grandma settled down, I was a bit of a storm-chaser.'

'Can we talk about you as a young man later, Grandpa,' said Lizzie. She was impatient to find out more about Dr Lancing. Grandpa loved telling her stories about his younger days and she usually loved hearing them, but today ... today was different.

'I'm getting to him, I'm getting to him. You need to hear this first,' he said.

'OK,' Lizzie sighed. 'What's a storm-chaser anyway?'

'It's a bit like a train-spotter but instead of travelling all over the place to watch trains, you go to where the big storms are forecast, and I mean big storms with funnel clouds, tornadoes, thunder and lightning. I found myself heading

45

more and more often to Macimanito.'

'But didn't you live here then?'

'No, no, no. Don't you remember me telling you? My folks were from a small farming community about a hundred miles north of here. That's where I met your grandma. Anyway, it made no sense to keep coming south to watch these amazing storms so I persuaded your grandma that we should come and live here, which we did in the 1960s.'

'But wasn't it dangerous living in a place with such severe weather conditions?' said Lizzie.

'Well, that was the odd thing. When the storms came, the worst of the weather always seemed to settle above the city centre. It sits in a hollowed-out bowl of a valley. Most of the residential areas were built on top of the escarpment surrounding the city so they escaped the destructive effects of the weather.

'The Mayor at the time, Alfred Klein, wanted to develop the city into a modern, 20th century business centre. He knew that any new buildings would have to be strong enough to withstand a regular pummelling from the storms and keep the people inside safe and warm. That's where Dr Lancing came in. Mayor Klein had read about his work. He'd been making a name for himself in Europe, designing public structures which could stand up to fierce storms, so he brought him over for talks.'

'Oh yes,' interrupted Lizzie. 'I remember reading something about that in the secret passage.'

'Secret passage?' said her grandpa.

'Yes. Never mind. I'll tell you later. What were you saying?'

'Mayor Klein persuaded the local council to commission Dr Lancing to completely remodel the city centre, using his technical and architectural know-how. I think it was the biggest project Dr Lancing had ever been asked to undertake. He brought over a team of designers and engineers from Europe to assist him in the preliminary studies and design work.

'Several years later, I remember the first skyscrapers going up and then the Skyway started to take shape. There was a lot of controversy over the years about which of the older buildings should be saved, and which should be demolished to make way for the new ones. Although some people disagreed with what was going on, they all seemed relieved when the Skyway was finally opened, and the violent storms miraculously stopped.'

'They stopped?'

'Yes. The local newspaper ran an article tracing the history of the most violent storms over recent years. It was only then that everyone realised we hadn't experienced any severe weather since the day the Skyway opened.'

'That's odd. Didn't anyone ask why?' said Lizzie.

'There was a lot of speculation at the time about whether there was a connection, but then everyone forgot about it.'

'What happened to Dr Lancing?'

'Oh, he stayed on. This was his biggest and most prestigious project. It made him a very wealthy man. I guess he wanted to stay close to the place that had made him a household name worldwide. The big businesses that set up in Macimanito, Gildchrist Corporation, Mountjoy Developments, Alba Oil and the rest of them, used to ask him to be guest speaker at their annual dinners. He gave lectures on the Skyway at universities all over the world.

'Then he died. Quite suddenly, poor chap.'

'How?'

'It was all a bit of a mystery to be honest. He was quite old by then. The newspapers said he died when lightning struck the communications tower. But it doesn't make sense. The tower, the Skyway, the whole city was built like one huge Faraday cage, to conduct lightning safely to ground. That was the whole point of Lancing's design.'

'So, the storms came back?' said Lizzie.

'Oh yes. They'd returned by then. The storms were nowhere near as often or as ferocious as before, but we saw a resurgence in the ten years or so prior to Dr Lancing's death. In fact, there was a massive thunderstorm the night you were born.'

'If he died in 2011,' Lizzie said, 'then his office must have been empty for nine years.'

'Where did you say you found it?'

'Along a secret passage in the blue sector of the Skyway. There was this sculpture in a glass cabinet and my hand sort of went through the glass and touched something and a door opened.'

'How very strange. I seem to recall your grandma saying something similar happened to her, but I can't quite remember wh ...'

'What's even stranger,' said Lizzie, who wasn't listening to him, 'is that Dr Lancing's office was a secret and that he built the Skyway in the shape of a pentagram.'

'I can't imagine why he kept his office a secret. Once the city had been rebuilt, his contract with the council ended so he wouldn't have had an office in the city. Unless he was asked to stay on of course. He did have a house in the north west of the city I believe. As to the shape of the Skyway ... maths was never my strong point at school ...' Grandpa's voice trailed off as tiredness overcame him and his head slowly slumped forward.

'Thanks Grandpa,' said Lizzie. She affectionately kissed

him on his forehead and tucked a woollen blanket round him.

'Is that you, Lizzie?' Her mum poked her head round the door.

'Sshhh!' Lizzie replied, holding a finger to her lips. 'He's just nodded off.'

'Close the door then and come with me.'

Lizzie followed her mum down the hallway towards the back room that looked out over the garden. Her mum opened the door and …

'SURPRISE!!!'

Lizzie's friends, relatives and neighbours greeted the birthday girl. A brightly coloured banner bearing the words

Lizzie Chambers is Thirteen!
Happy Birthday!

was suspended from the curtain pole. Balloons wobbled on the ceiling, party poppers popped. In the middle of the room a table was laden with sandwiches, crisps, muffins, cakes and biscuits.

'Happy birthday my darling girl,' her mum said, giving her a squeeze and a kiss on the cheek.

'Thanks Mum,' said Lizzie. 'All my favourite food!'

Lizzie tried to sound enthusiastic for her mum's sake.

She hadn't wanted a fuss on her birthday. She hated being the centre of attention. But she knew that both her mum and grandpa liked to indulge her, and she couldn't blame them for wanting to make an occasion of such an important birthday. She'd reached a milestone in her life.

Thirteen! Six years of being a teenager to look forward to. Is that a cause for celebration or not?

She sidled up to Josh who was stuffing his face with birthday cake at one end of the table.

'You knew about this?'

'Yupph!' he replied, his cheeks puffed out like a hamster's.

'You could have told me.'

'No s'prise then. Nom nom.'

'Well don't let me keep you from your food,' she said, 'but tomorrow we have to go back to the Skyway.'

'Nom nom Noooo!'

'Listen, munchkins. Grandpa told me about Dr Lancing. We need to get to the bottom of why the Skyway was really built. I'll come around to your place at six o'clock tomorrow morning, sharp. OK?'

Still busy chewing, Josh gave her the thumbs-up.

THE SKYWAY

At 3.32am precisely, Lizzie finally gave up trying to sleep. She switched on the red lamp on her desk, opened a notebook and picked up a pencil.

She drew a line down the middle of a blank page, making two columns.

Facts	Questions
Dr Lancing built the Skyway to protect the city from storms	Why are there so many storms over the city? Why did they stop when the Skyway was built? Why did they return years later?
He kept a secret office off the Skyway	Why? How did we manage to get in?
He needed new transponders for the pods	What are the pods? Why did they need new transponders? What have pods & transponders got to do with the Skyway?

He left the office on 15 June 2011 in a hurry.	Why? Why did he not come back?
A natural disaster is heading for the city (?)	Why, what sort and when will it happen?
My birth chart numbers are 4,5,7,8 (?)	Why are they important? How will they help me stop the disaster?

Not sure if those last two facts are actually facts. More like unproven theories.

Now for the questions. Uurgh, there're so many of them!

Writing everything down had at least cleared her mind. Or so she thought. Climbing back into bed she tried to doze off. It was no use. She started making a list in her head of all the things she needed to take with her later that morning.

would

Notebook and pen. Torch and spare batteries. Compass, in case we get really lost ...

She eventually drifted off. When she next opened her eyes, the clock said 5.45am.

Yikes! Time to go!

Lizzie sprang out of bed, threw off her pyjamas and dressed in what looked like miniature army fatigues. They were a birthday present from her mum, She had agreed to her daughter's rather unusual request, deciding it was simply a phase she was going through.

who

Lizzie tried to remember all the stuff she had to pack, and started filling her pockets. Lying on a chair in the corner of the room were two pieces of thin rope she'd been practising tying knots with. *Better take them as well.*

What else, what else? She tapped her chin with her index finger. 'Ah yes!' she said, picking up the Swiss army knife from the shelf by the door.

Looping the spearhead necklace round her neck and grabbing her rucksack, she quietly descended the staircase and pulled on her trainers and winter jacket. She moved into the kitchen and opened the fridge door. Despite Josh's best attempts to clear the table of food at her party, there were still some left-over sandwiches, biscuits and cake. Lizzie slipped these into a plastic bag and then into her rucksack. She hastily scribbled a note to her mum - 'Gone to Josh's' - which she placed on the kitchen table before leaving quietly by the front door.

Five minutes later Lizzie was at Josh's house wondering how to wake him up without rousing the entire family. She had studied with him enough times to know that his bedroom was at the back of the house, so she walked round the side of the building and gently lifted the latch on the gate. Their back garden comprised a small patch of grass with a garage at the end facing out towards a lane. She picked up a stone from one of the flower borders and threw it at the window on the right. No response. *Come on Josh - wake up you lazy so-and-so.* She picked up another, bigger stone this time and hurled it at the window.

CHINK!

The pebble bounced off the glass. She waited. A face appeared at the window.

Josh opened it wide and poked his head out into the cold, morning air. His eyes were half closed, his hair stuck out in all directions. 'Oh, it's you,' he said.

'Yes, it's me. Get up; we need to get going,' she whispered urgently.

'But it's only ....' He moved back inside to look at the clock on his bedside table, 'six o'clock'.

'The Skyway never sleeps. Come on, look sharp,' said Lizzie.

'OK, OK,' said Josh wearily. 'I'll let you in.'

Moments later, Lizzie heard a key turning in the back door. It opened to reveal Josh standing there in dishevelled black pyjamas printed all over with red flames.

'Mmm - like the jim jams!' Lizzie snorted, stepping into their kitchen.

'Yeah well, whatever. Stay here and I'll be down in a minute.'

Josh headed back upstairs, rubbing his face with his hands to wake up. He went to the bathroom and splashed water on his face. Back in his room, he pulled on whatever clothes he could find on the floor.

As he headed back down the stairs, the muffled voice of his mother said, 'Is that you Josh?' from the direction of his parents' bedroom.

'Yeah - I'm just going to Lizzie's. We've got a project to finish off for school tomorrow.'

'But it's so early,' his mum protested half-heartedly, too befuddled with sleep to really take in what he was saying.

Josh didn't bother to reply. He knew his mum and dad enjoyed a lie-in at the weekend and wouldn't be up for another couple of hours. He could hear his younger brother Dan, who was only six, playing with his toys in his bedroom.

As he entered the kitchen, Josh noticed Lizzie's combat gear for the first time.

'Whoa! What are you wearing?'

'Do you like them?' she said, standing up and giving him a twirl. 'I asked Mum to buy them for my birthday.'

'Well they're certainly different - for a girl. Expecting to go into battle or something?'

'That's not the point. They're hard-wearing, functional, and have lots of pockets where I can put things,' she said. She tore open the Velcro flap of a pouch on the right calf of her trousers. Inserting a hand, she pulled out the Swiss army knife to show him.

'So why the rucksack?'

'Provisions. I've brought some of the left-overs from the party yesterday.'

Josh's eyes lit up. 'What about drinks? Here - add these to your stash,' he said, grabbing two bottles of fizzy drink from the fridge. 'They can be my contribution.'

'Right, we're all set. Come on!'

Josh hurriedly dragged on his trainers and jacket and followed Lizzie out the back door.

The previous day's storm had abated during the night, leaving a chilly, crystalline quality to the air. The city felt cleansed. On their way to the station, Lizzie told Josh what her grandpa had said about Dr Lancing.

'It was pretty random the way we found his office. How did you manage to open that door?'

'I've been thinking about that. You remember those sea creatures made of glass?'

'Yes.'

'Well they each had a line of bumps on their backs - there were seven on the jellyfish, four on the sea urchin, eight on the squid and ....'

'Five on the other fish?' Josh finished her sentence.

'Exactly! My numbers! I must have touched them in a certain sequence and that's what triggered the mechanism that opened the door.'

'That doesn't explain how you put your hand through

the sides of the glass display cabinet.'

'No, it doesn't,' agreed Lizzie. She wished she'd been more patient and listened to Grandpa when he'd said something similar had happened to her grandma.

'Maybe you've got magical powers after all......Oooo!' He lifted up his hands and wiggled his fingers in front of Lizzie's face.'

'Ha, very funny!' said Lizzie, swiping at him. His words made her uneasy. She felt something scratching away at her consciousness, trying to break through. She sent it away with a shake of her head.

They disembarked when the Z-train reached the Gildchrist building entrance to the Skyway. This marked the most westerly point of the downtown area of the city.

'Do you remember the model of the Skyway in Dr Lancing's office?' said Lizzie, 'and that it was in the shape of a five-pointed star? Well I reckon we are standing on one of the points. If the shape is significant then this seems like a good place to start looking.'

They entered the lobby of the building and looked around for a Skyway sign. In the centre of the vast space, a glass lift shaft encrusted with diamante crystals rose skyward. Steel bridges with mirrored undersides radiated out from the glistening column to the floors above. A sheet of water trickled down a vertical wall of shimmering steel on one side of them. On another, foliage cascaded down from a great height creating a veil of emerald green. The floor on which they stood was made of white marble shot through with veins of turquoise and vermilion.

'What is this place?' said Lizzie.

'It's the headquarters of the Gildchrist Corporation,' said Josh. 'A friend of my dad's works for them. They mine for diamonds in the far north. Very successful too, I hear. They set up their headquarters here in the mid-1980s.'

'Wow!'

'Can I help you?' said a surly security man seated at the reception desk that stretched the width of the lobby.

'We're looking for the entrance to the Skyway,' said Josh.

'Over there,' the man pointed to his right. 'Take the escalator to the first-floor corridor and follow the signs.'

'Thank you!' they both said and made their way upstairs.

At the top, four corridors stretched off into the distance.

'Can I have something to eat before we decide which way to go,' said Josh pleadingly. 'You didn't give me a chance to have any breakfast.'

'Oh alright, if you must. But we've got more important

things to think about than your stomach, you know.'

'Well you can do the thinking while I do the eating.' He plonked himself on the floor next to a fern in a large silver pot, which stood against the wall of the circular landing area. Lizzie took the hint and sat beside him, swinging the rucksack off her back and on to the floor beside her.

'Cheese and pickle or ham and tomato?' asked Lizzie.

'Ham and tomato, please. And some crisps. And something to drink.'

'Anything else Sir?' Lizzie said.

'No - that'll do for now, thank you very much.' He unwrapped his sandwich and slumped heavily against the potted plant. There was a sharp click and the pot shifted slightly revealing a gap in the floor beneath it.

'What on earth ......?' He didn't have time to finish his sentence before the pot moved again and a much bigger hole opened up. Caught off balance, he felt himself falling sideways and instinctively grabbed Lizzie's arm. Together they tumbled sideways into the pitch blackness.

KITCHI

Kitchi stood on the escarpment overlooking Macimanito. The city had grown to fill the circular hollow in the earth it had claimed one hundred and fifty years previously. Where once low-rise wooden buildings had populated the downtown area, there were now towering edifices of concrete, steel and glass. Monuments to the successful businesses that had grown in the city. It was a curious sight, this futuristic cityscape, sunk in the pitted scar of an otherwise unblemished flat, prairie land. Curiouser still was the slender, tapered spire of the communications tower at the very centre of the city. A shining, metallic shard that loomed above everything else, like the finger of a vengeful robot pointing accusingly heavenward. Virtually all that remained of the original city was the road system, much extended over the years. It was organised as a grid of roads running at right angles to each other, east to west and north to south.

He wondered what his ancestors would have thought about the transformation of their sacred land into this shiny man-made city. In his dreams, he had seen someone not unlike himself, younger perhaps, with black hair, dressed in buffalo skins, enter a medicine lodge in the valley. There he cut his chest with a long knife and beat himself with aspen branches in a ritual to appease the gods. The Takoda had known this was a special place. A place where the gods of earth and heaven came together to battle each other, bringing with them ferocious storms that drove their people away.

European settlers had had no such qualms. Pleased to find a piece of land on the main east-west trade route where the First People did not want to live, they had started building a town. In their arrogance, they thought they could live there without fear of electrical storms, mighty whirlwinds and tumultuous rain. They had been wrong. For decades, they endured vicious storms until Dr Lancing built the Skyway. But the beast was still there, lying in wait under the city.

Kitchi scanned the city skyline. From his vantage point he could clearly make out Lancing's pentagram, the tips of the five-pointed star marked by iconic office buildings. To the west was Gildchrist's golden chevron, to the south the mirrored sail of Mountjoy Developments and in the east the copper roof of Chen's pagoda-shaped office block. He was one of a select few who knew that beneath these structures lay Lancing's answer to Macimanito's infernal power, a power that threatened to destroy the city.

A gentle breeze caressed Kitchi's cheek. Its cooling effect soothed the scar tissue that covered the left side of his face. Twisted, red flesh where once an eyeball had been, extended along his cheek, down his jaw line and on to his neck. He brought up his claw-like left hand to his face and gently touched it, remembering the explosion and fire that had killed his friend Dr Lancing. Kitchi had tried desperately to save him, to snatch him from the jaws of the inferno, but it had consumed Harold like a rapacious dragon and almost taken Kitchi as well. Most of his hair had been burned off and when it grew back it was completely white, as if purified in a baptism of fire thrown down by the gods.

Kitchi was the only surviving member of the original team entrusted with remodelling Macimanito. Mayor Klein, recognising the sensitivities involved in building a modern city on First People's land, had asked Kitchi to work with Dr Lancing to ensure they acknowledged his people's culture appropriately. As an educated, pure blood Takoda, Kitchi had become the leader of the First People's Council and as such was a natural choice.

Closing his eyes and taking a deep breath, Kitchi ceased his reverie and made his way down the path that led into the city. Having lost a dear friend as well as a colleague in Dr Lancing, he felt he owed it to Harold to continue supporting his work on the Skyway. Reggie Grant and his team had taken over following Harold's death.

Reggie had asked Kitchi to check out a few of the pods and report back anything unusual. It could have waited until Monday, but Kitchi was restless and needed a walk so he decided to take a look at the pods on his day off.

The grassy slopes surrounding the gravel path that led to the outskirts of town sparkled in the morning sun as light reflected off the frosted blades. They made a satisfying crunch when Kitchi's boot accidentally strayed from the path. The bare branches of spindly trees trembled in the wind as if they, too, could feel the cold. There wasn't another soul about. A patch of uneven ground where tree roots had pushed up from below, cracking the tarmac, caused Kitchi to take his hands out of his coat pockets to steady himself. As he did so, a flat, ivory-coloured object slid down his rough textured coat and landed silently in the grass. Unnoticed by Kitchi, it caught the attention of a shadowy figure crouching behind a rocky outcrop a few hundred yards away. The path eventually opened out on to a pavement as the first houses came into view.

A profound sadness overcame Kitchi when he saw the grand, three-storey mansion on the corner. This had been Dr Lancing's house. He and a few other confidantes had met with the great man here on numerous occasions to discuss the findings of the initial surveys, to plan next steps and to celebrate when the Skyway had been opened. It was here that Macimanito's secret had been revealed. Dr Lancing had invited some of the world's top engineers to help him create a city that could not only withstand the monster, but also tame it.

The stone house was distinguished by a tall, octagonal turret with a roof clad in terracotta, fish-scale-shaped tiles, that rose above an imposing entrance supported on four columns. Steps led up to the front door which still bore the initials 'H.L.' etched into the glass panel in its upper half. The rest of the house seemed to emanate out from the turret. A large, glass conservatory on one side, an enormous bay window on the other. The rooms stretched out towards the back of the building. All the curtains were drawn. The house had been left unoccupied after Lancing's death. As he walked past, he caught a glimpse of the red roof of the playhouse in the back garden. He remembered looking out from one of the windows and seeing a little girl running in and out of it, laughing as she went, her dark curls bobbing behind her.

Lizzie was a bright little thing even then, he thought to himself, before heading into the city towards the gleaming tower of the Gildchrist building.

POD NUMBER ONE

'Oomph!' Lizzie landed with a thump on top of Josh, knocking the air out of him and squashing the ham and tomato sandwich into his neck. Embarrassed, she got up, dusted herself off and switched on the torch she'd pulled from her pocket. She shone it in Josh's face.

'You idiot! Why did you pull me down with you?'

Josh was busy picking food from under his chin and shoving it in his mouth.

'Unbelievable! How can you think about food at a time like this?'

'It's awright for shum!' he said, 'I cushioned your fall!' He'd landed awkwardly on some sandbags at the bottom of the chute. 'I need to lie here a minute and recover.'

'Stuff your face you mean!'

'Well, I was hungry and still am. Where are those crisps?'

Lizzie made a sweep of the floor with her torch. She spotted a mess of broken crisps and bits of bread. 'Bad news, buddy. Looks like the bag broke on the way down.'

'Ahhh! That is so disappointing!'

'Come on. Up you get! Let's look around.' Lizzie was feeling impatient and had little sympathy for her friend.

Josh pushed up from the floor with his one free hand, still munching. He followed Lizzie.

'Can you smell that?' she said. 'It reminds me of that time you singed your hair over the Bunsen burner.'

She scanned the area with her torch. They'd fallen into a round, concrete chamber in the middle of which stood a huge, solid-looking, metal object bolted to the floor. It was painted bright yellow. Two enormous flattened U-shaped lumps of metal were positioned one upside down on top of the other so there was a gaping hole in the middle. Nestled inside were identically shaped but slightly smaller pieces of metal. Streaming away from the outside edge of the upper and lower sections were rows of opaque orange tubes. They disappeared into the distance on either side like the wayward hair of a faceless giant. A grey metal box in front of the object housed what looked like a control panel with a series of dials. They all registered zero.

Josh, who had finally finished eating, said: 'What on earth is it?'

'It's some sort of machine. You see those tubes coming out of it? Well, if you look closely,' she said, moving her torch inches from the plastic tubing, 'you can see wires running through them. Maybe they're power cables.'

They walked around the object, ducking under the array of tubes, which ran horizontally at head height. On the other side, Lizzie noticed that the pale grey of the concrete floor and wall had been stained a sooty black. The mangled, charred remains of a control box lay on the floor, spilling out wires, circuit boards and components. Beside it a lone boot stood watching them, its sole melted to the spot.

'There must have been a fire.' Lizzie examined the stain. It seemed to take on a human shape the longer she looked at it. 'Oh yuck! That's what the smell is. It's not just burnt hair, it's probably burnt bodies as well. Why else would that boot be there?'

In the torch light a pair of eyes shone back at them.

'Whoa!' Josh and Lizzie instinctively took a step back, their hearts racing.

'Meow!' A thin little cry split the air.

Lizzie's torch illuminated a black ball of fluff hunkered inside the boot, only its eyes and one ear showing.

'Naughty kitty!' she scolded the cat, 'you gave us such a fright.' She bent down to pick her up, but Celeste was having none of it. She sprang out of her temporary bed and headed off into the darkness.

'Let's follow her. See where she goes,' said Lizzie.

'Why?' queried Josh.

'Well, for a cat to be down here it must know the way in and the way out. Unless you were planning on scrabbling back up that chute.'

'Mmm. I suppose you're right,' Josh agreed reluctantly, 'but anything or anyone could be here. It's so dark. We wouldn't see them until they're really close.'

'Don't be ridiculous Josh. There's no-one here. We'd hear them. Now come on; we need to be quick before puss disappears altogether.'

Lizzie took the lead, holding the torch so they could see where they were going. They followed the wall as it curved round a bend. The chamber narrowed into a long corridor. Along the centre ran a horizontal metal rack supporting the dozens of tubes coming from the yellow machine. On and on they walked, keeping the cat in sight, until they arrived at another chamber with an identical machine at its centre. A few hundred metres later they came to another and then another.

They came to a stop in the fourth chamber. 'They're all

connected, whatever they are,' said Lizzie. She kept an eye on Celeste, who was sitting on the floor licking her shoulder.

'Maybe it's some sort of electrical power distribution network,' said Josh. 'You know, to control the lighting and heating in the Skyway and office buildings.'

'But surely it would be on right now if that were the case,' said Lizzie. 'The dials in the first chamber were all set at zero.'

'Yes, but it's just possible that...'

'Sshhh!' Lizzie cut Josh off.

The distant sound of softly running footsteps resonated off the sides of the chamber. Every so often there was a pause in the steps followed by a 'thunk'.

'There's someone coming,' Lizzie whispered urgently. 'We've got to hide.'

'There's nowhere to hide,' said Josh, panicking.

'Yes, there is. Quick. Inside the machine.'

Before Josh could object, Lizzie started climbing into the yawning mouth of the yellow contraption. Josh clambered in after her.

'I don't think this is a very good idea,' he whispered. 'What happens if someone turns this thing on?'

'We don't even know what it is. If it's dangerous there would be warning signs around the place wouldn't there?'

'Not if it's a secret!' said Josh.

Lizzie hadn't thought of that. Maybe she should start listening to Josh occasionally, instead of bulldozing his ideas all the time and not giving him a chance to speak.

They huddled together against one side of the gap.

The running steps came closer and closer, and then stopped. There was a sharp click and then a 'thunk' as the strip light on the ceiling flickered into life. Black and yellow warning signs on the wall opposite said 'Danger: strong electro-magnetic field. When red light flashes, evacuate immediately.'

Lizzie and Josh stayed perfectly still and quiet.

'I wouldn't stay in there if I were you,' a familiar voice intoned. 'It could be very dangerous. Didn't I warn you not to go exploring the Skyway?'

Kitchi walked slowly to the front of the machine where they could see him.

As his damaged features came into view Lizzie and Josh flinched involuntarily, but they couldn't take their eyes off him. They froze.

'Out with you then. You two have some explaining to do.'

THE PENTAGRAM

Kitchi had known there was something wrong as soon as he'd entered Pod Number One. A needle of light had threaded its way down the ventilation shaft, throwing a silvery trail across the floor of the darkened chamber.

Someone or something had moved the cover of the shaft. He picked up a long metal pole with a hook at one end. Reaching up, he pulled the lid shut. The automatic closing mechanism had malfunctioned.

He switched on the overhead strip light and looked around. At the bottom of the shaft lay a mess of broken crisps and bits of bread and tomato. They're here, he thought to himself, and unless they know how to find the exits in the dark they can't have gone far.

With no time to waste, Kitchi had run around the length of the corridor from chamber to chamber, switching on the overhead lights as he went until he'd finally caught up with them. Their urgent whispering had given them away.

***

Lizzie and Josh reluctantly climbed off the machine and stood facing Kitchi.

'You're the man from the Z-train,' said Lizzie matter-of-factly. 'What are you doing here?'

THWACK! Josh kicked Lizzie's boot.

'I might ask you the same thing,' said Kitchi.

He picked up Celeste and ran his hand along her back. A sonorous purr started deep in her throat.

'You saw the blackened wall in the pod where you landed? The charred control box?' he said, not taking his eyes off the cat.

'Yes.'

'Well that's what happened to the previous outsiders who thought they could solve our problems. We asked for scientists, engineers with special talents. Those who came were amateurs, codebreakers, enthusiasts. They had no real knowledge or understanding of the power that is unleashed by the beast beneath this city. We let them try, but they paid the price, as did this little one.' Kitchi stroked

Celeste's head where her second ear should have been.

'Beast?' said Josh nervously. 'What beast?'

'And what problems?' said Lizzie, curious to hear more. She liked the idea of solving problems.

'Enough for now,' Kitchi said, ignoring their questions, his voice taking on a weary tone. 'At least you're safe down here for the moment. No storms are forecast for today and the electro-magnets are switched off.'

Lizzie's mind raced as she tried to pull together all the pieces of information they had learned about the Skyway - the Golden Ratio, Dr Lancing's accident, the storms and now electro-magnets. But how did they all fit together?

'You haven't explained what you're doing here,' said Kitchi, starting to walk in the direction they'd been going.

'Well, I was sitting next to a potted plant on the Skyway landing, about to eat a sandwich, when ....'

'I know *how* you fell into the chamber,' Kitchi interrupted Josh. 'What were you doing snooping round in the first place?'

'We weren't *snooping*,' said Lizzie. She felt rather insulted. Snooping suggested something dishonest. 'We were *exploring!*'

'And what, exactly, did you hope to find?'

'Well that's just it ...' said Josh in an exasperated tone.

Lizzie turned to him with narrowed eyes and a look

that would have stopped a herd of rampaging buffalo. The last thing she wanted was for him to blurt everything out to this stranger.

Information is power. Who said that? Probably a scientist. Let's see what he can tell us first.

'I'm doing some research for a school science project…'

About what? Think, think!

'To do with the heat insulating properties of different materials. I've been measuring the temperature in different parts of the Skyway.'

'I see.' The stranger didn't seem convinced.

'And what about your friend?'

'Josh, you mean? Oh, I had to bring someone. My mum won't let me go into town by myself.'

'Thanks!' said Josh huffily.

Whoops! Engage brain before opening mouth.

'He's also my science buddy at school and he's really clever.'

Josh nodded sagely.

'Where are you taking us?' said Lizzie. She suddenly realised they didn't know where they were going whether they could trust this strange-looking man.

'I'm taking you out of here,' said Kitchi. 'But first I thought you might like to view the inner sanctum. Given

76

that you've already seen some of the pods in the array.'

'PODS!' Josh mouthed to Lizzie.

'What is a pod?' he said.

'POD is an acronym for Pentagram Operational Device. The curved chambers housing each electro-magnet are positioned relative to each other at the points of a five-pointed star, or pentagram.'

'Oh!' said Lizzie, slapping her forehead. 'Like the model of the Skyway we saw in ... Whoops!' Lizzie realised she had said too much. Josh rolled his eyes in exasperation.

'The model of the Skyway?' said Kitchi abruptly. 'But there was only one model made and that was in ... Where did you see it?'

'Dr Lancing's office,' Lizzie whispered, shrinking from the large man with the scarred face and white hair bearing down on her.

Not even Kitchi knew how to gain access to Lancing's old office. The code to get in was the same as the one lost when Lancing died. If Lizzie had been in Lancing's office, she must know the code.

Startled by the man's angry response, Josh tried to deflate the situation by changing the subject.

'Dr Galloway told us all about pentagrams and the Golden Ratio,' he offered.

'Yyy...es,' said Lizzie. Her courage gone, she hoped the

man would back away from her.

Kitchi had not meant to frighten the youngsters. He sometimes forgot how scary he looked, especially when agitated.

'Ah, Maurice!' he said, trying to soften the rasp in his voice caused by a scorched windpipe.

'Do you know Dr Galloway?' said Lizzie. She was encouraged by Kitchi's gentler tone.

'He and I had a lot of fun at school together, especially in science class. Afterwards I studied geophysics at college whereas he chose to teach - such a waste!'

'It's not a waste ....' started Josh, springing to his favourite teacher's defence.

'My father was a geophysicist,' said Lizzie.

'I know. We worked together. Don't you remember me at all Lizzie? I'm Kitchi. Kitchi Nosky. You must have been about three or four years old when you used to play in Dr Lancing's garden. Your father brought you along to our meetings sometimes when your mother was busy.'

Lizzie was confused. She studied the undamaged half of his face, then the other side, searching for any semblance of familiarity.

Dr Lancing's garden …

A glimmer of a memory surfaced. Running around and around on a wide, grassy lawn in between trees and bushes, laughing. A small outbuilding with a red roof. At the window of the big house a man's face, watching. Sharp, angular features, dark eyes and skin, long black hair. *Could that have been him?*

'Your father and I started working together the year you were born. As part of the team monitoring the geological sub-strata of rocks underneath the city. I knew him for about six years until ....'

'Until he died,' said Lizzie. 'Out in Africa somewhere."

'Y... yes, yes. That's ... that's right,' he said hesitantly.

Kitchi knew this wasn't true. But it wasn't his place to dispel whatever myth Lizzie's mother had spun about Charles Chambers' death.

Lizzie felt herself warm to this stranger, despite his abrupt manner and scary face.

He knew my father! He might be able to tell me more about him. Things I don't know. About his work as a scientist.

'Anyway,' said Kitchi. 'Here we are.'

He released Celeste on to the floor and pressed the palm of his right hand against the wall. A door slid open. They entered a short, narrow corridor leading to a circular chamber. In the middle sat five huge, black machines in a row. They looked like gigantic, fat worms. A bank of dials and switches covered most of the wall.

'Wow! Where are we?' asked Lizzie.

'We are at the very centre of the pentagram,' said Kitchi. 'These,' he said, gesturing to the machines, 'are electrical generators. When they're switched on by remote control from the communications tower, they send a massive electrical current through the electro-magnets, creating an electro-magnetic field. The magnets are arranged in such a way that the electro-magnetic field is concentrated down into the earth beneath the city.'

'But isn't that incredibly dangerous?' asked Josh.

'It can be, if you don't know what you're doing.'

'But why ...?'

Kitchi raised his hand to silence her. A persistent banging sound had started up somewhere in the distance.

'That sounds like trouble. Quick. Let's get you out of here.

QUID PRO QUO

Lizzie spotted the bedraggled looking man as they rounded a corner of the Skyway a few minutes after leaving Kitchi. From a distance, he looked like a bundle of rags.

'Spare change?' he said, holding out a dirty hand from the sleeve of his ill-fitting jacket.

'Sorry - we don't have any,' she said, barely breaking stride. Her mum had warned her not to give money to street people.

Lizzie wrinkled her nose in anticipation of the peculiar, pungent odour she associated with vagrants. It never came. Instead she detected the faint scent of lilacs.

'Oh, please miss, young sir, just a few pennies?' the man said. 'I can make it worth your while.'

Josh, until then too lost in his own thoughts to even register the man, stopped and turned to look at him.

'What did you say?'

'I can make it worth your while.' The man gave him a simpering look.

'Come on. We're wasting our time here.'

Lizzie strode off with Josh in her wake.

'Wouldn't you like to know the secret of the Skyway?' the man shouted after them.

Lizzie stopped. She turned to look at the man.

'What do you mean?'

'I know someone who can tell you all about the Skyway.'

Lizzie and Josh looked at each other. They brought their heads together.

'What do you think?' Lizzie whispered.

'I think he looks dodgy.'

'But what if he does know something?'

'What if he's a murderer or a cannibal and we are his next victims.'

'Don't be ridiculous, Josh. You've been watching too many horror movies.'

'I'm not being ridiculous. Did you see his beady black eyes and that little pink mouth through his straggly beard?'

'So?'

'So - he gives me the creeps.'

'Everyone gives you the creeps.'

'No, they don't. Besides, there's something not right with him. He doesn't smell like a street person.'

'I noticed that too!'

'So?'

'So ... what's the worst thing that could happen?'

'We could die!'

'Statistically that's not very likely. In this part of the world murder represents less than one percent of violent crime ....'

'Or he could beat us up!'

'Honestly Josh. You're such a scaredy cat! We're here to explore the Skyway. We know about the electro-magnets but not why they're there. He may be our best chance of finding out. If we stick together, we'll be fine.'

'But he could be lying!'

'We'll never know unless we go with him.'

'This doesn't feel right, Lizzie!'

'If you don't want to go with me ...'

Josh sighed.... 'Do I have a choice?'

Lizzie smiled. 'Not really?'

'OK then.'

Phew! Thank goodness he's coming.

Despite claiming to be fearless, Lizzie was a little scared.

But not as scared as she was curious.

We just need to stay safe. How do we do that? Stay together. Don't let him take us anywhere it's dark and there's no-one around. Watch out for accomplices. Be prepared to defend ourselves and/or run like crazy.

If all goes well, we'll discover the secret of the Skyway, where my numbers fit in and how I can save the city. Yay! But why would he tell us. What's in it for him? Mmm …

'OK. We'll go with you,' Lizzie said to the man. 'On one condition.'

'Anything you ask, young lady.'

'Stay ten feet in front of us at all times.' Lizzie looked at Josh and raised her eyebrows as if to say, 'will that keep you happy?'

'OK. Follow me.'

The man shuffled off along the Skyway. He occasionally turned his head to make sure Lizzie and Josh were following him.

'I'm still not sure about this,' whispered Josh to Lizzie out of the side of his mouth.

'Don't worry,' Lizzie whispered back. 'Keep your eyes open in case he has any associates, in which case we'll split up and run for it. Right now, there are two of us and only one of him. If he makes a move on us, I'll kick him in the shins, and you punch him between the legs. That'll bring him down.'

Josh winced. He wondered where his friend had learned self-defence.

After several changes of direction, they found themselves back where they had started that morning; on an upper floor of the Gildchrist building.

'We need to go down the escalator, through security and then up to the top,' said the man. 'I'm afraid the elevator is barely ten feet wide, so I may have to stand a little closer to you than you'd like.'

The man used a pass to get through the security turnstile.

'Hello there!' said a rotund man behind the reception desk. He was wearing a black uniform with 'security' embossed on the chest pocket. The watcher scowled at him.

'So,' said Lizzie quietly. 'He must work here.'

'Why is he dressed like a street person then?' said Josh.

They walked across the white marble floor and into the elevator. A few minutes later they arrived at the twenty-first floor. Stepping out of the lift, their feet sank into plush lilac carpeting. Its colour and luxuriousness reflected the delicate scent of flowers in the air. Floor to ceiling windows framed a spectacular cityscape on one side and a view of the endless prairie on the other.

'Wow!' Lizzie and Josh couldn't help being impressed.

Their companion pushed open the crystal-encrusted double doors in front of them and ushered them into what looked like a waiting area. Deep purple leather sofas lined the walls. At the centre of the room stood a diamond-shaped glass coffee table neatly piled with glossy magazines.

'Take a seat,' said the watcher, gesturing for them to sit. 'I won't be a moment.'

Lizzie and Josh did as they were asked. The man spoke in quiet tones to the smartly dressed woman sitting behind a large, white oak desk to one side of the room.

'Luckily for you, she's in. She needed to sign some contracts before tomorrow,' she said.

They watched as the woman entered the white door behind her. She re-emerged.

'In you go,' she said to the man.

Moments later they heard raised voices coming from the office, muffled by the thickness of the door.

'What's going on?' asked Josh quietly. 'No idea, but it doesn't sound good,' replied Lizzie.

'BRRR, BRRR BRRR!'

The woman sitting behind the desk picked up the phone.

'You can go in now,' she said.

Lizzie and Josh hesitated.

'Go on, in you go. She won't bite,' she urged.

Lizzie led the way. Josh followed a few steps behind her.

Entering the room, they took in the richness of their surroundings. The opulent desk, the picture windows, the glass and steel shelves, the crystal chandelier and table lamps. Their scruffy companion sat on a chair in one corner of the room looking sheepish. In the middle of the room stood a silver-haired woman in a sky-blue silk suit and white shirt. She smiled benignly at them with her arms outstretched.

'Come in, come in. Please sit. How nice to meet you both. My name is Toni. I understand that my man has brought you here under a bit of a pretext.'

'P...p...pretext,' said Josh nervously. 'What does that mean?'

'It means the reason he gave for bringing you here was not strictly true.'

'Not true?' Lizzie was outraged. 'But he said you would tell us the secret of the Skyway!'

'Oh, did he diddums?' Gildchrist stuck out her bottom lip, making fun of Lizzie, who glared at her.

'Do you really want to know the secret that badly?' she sneered. 'Well I'll tell you what; if you tell me something,

I'll tell you what you want to know. How about that?'

Lizzie was seething. How dare this flashy woman in her big, fancy office with her dolly-bird secretary make fun of her.

'Well?' Lizzie shouted, her face crumpling in anger. 'What do you want to know?'

'I believe you know how to get into a certain Dr Lancing's office,' Gildchrist said calmly. She started walking around Lizzie and Josh like a shark circling its prey.

'How do you know that?' asked Lizzie, twisting her head round so she could keep an eye on her.

'Why, my faithful man here,' she said, 'has been following you. He heard you talking when you re-emerged from that secret passage you found in the Skyway.'

'Why do you want to know? What have you got to do with Dr Lancing?'

'Let's just say I have a vested interest in his work. Particularly the surveys he conducted before and after building the Skyway.'

She wasn't going to divulge the real reason she wanted the code. Especially not to this impertinent young girl who had no respect for her elders. Gildchrist remembered when she was about Lizzie's age how her father had always been very particular when it came to good manners.

'Children should be seen and not heard,' he used to say, 'and the same goes for women.' If Gildchrist so much as scraped a knife across her plate at the dinner table, her father would drag her by one ear into a corner to face the wall. There she'd remain until the meal was over. 'She's only a little girl,' her mother would plead. His response was a resounding slap to the face. Gildchrist flinched at the memory.

'And you'll tell me the secret of the Skyway if I tell you the code to Dr Lancing's office?' said Lizzie.

'Of course, young lady, of course,' she said trying to sound sincere.

'Well I'm not telling you,' Lizzie shouted, slumping into a leather chair in front of the desk. Lizzie stared defiantly ahead, her arms tightly crossed. She was annoyed with herself for being duped so easily.

Gildchrist stopped circling and slammed a clenched fist against the wall, making the watcher jump in his seat. How dare she speak to her like that! Her father would have knocked six bells out of her if she'd so flagrantly disobeyed his wishes.

Josh had remained silent during this heated exchange. A rising panic started to burn in his chest.

'She doesn't mean that,' he spoke at last, sensing Gildchrist's agitation. 'Do you Lizzie?' He turned to his friend with a beseeching look on his face.

'Yes, I DO!' she said emphatically, not even looking at him.

'Right. Well there's only one thing for it,' said Gildchrist, rage simmering just below the surface. She picked up the gilt phone on her desk. 'Clarissa, call special services.'

'W... what are you doing,' said Josh, more nervous than ever.

'You'll see young man, you'll see.'

A few minutes later two huge men with mean faces and bald heads, dressed in long, brown leather coats entered the room.

'Put them in lock down,' instructed Gildchrist.

The two men walked over to Lizzie and Josh, picked them up and threw them over their shoulders like bags of flour. Josh froze, unable to move. Lizzie hammered the back of the man carrying her.

'Let me go, let me go!' she screamed as they left the office.

'Perhaps some thinking time will help you change your mind.'

THE MEETING

Toni Gildchrist curled her lip in distaste. She was flanked by three men on either side. Another six sat opposite. The long, rectangular mahogany table dominated the main meeting room at Electrix Towers, headquarters of the city's electrical supply company.

Look at them all, she thought.   Chief executives of Macimanito's leading businesses. Sitting there like animated man dolls, dressed identically in suits of varying shades of grey. They haven't an ounce of originality between them. Where are the visionaries, the trend-setters? Stuffed shirts the lot of them. Except Grant, of course.

Reggie Grant, undaunted by the suits, had come to the meeting dressed in overalls.

'Gentlemen, gentlemen!' Mayor Klimpton raised his voice to silence the chatter. 'And lady, of course.' He glanced at Gildchrist. 'I think it's time we began. Thank you all for attending this meeting of the Skyway Committee.'

'As you may be aware, a severe weather front is approaching our city. To put into perspective its potential impact, I have asked an expert from the meteorological office to give us a presentation on what we can expect.'

The Mayor picked up the phone in front of him and asked his secretary to show in Mr Yule. A few seconds later the door opened. A small, mole-like man with black hair, round glasses perched on the end of his nose and a greasy-looking dark jacket and trousers entered the room.

'Welcome Mr Yule, welcome!' the Mayor said effusively. 'Please sit down.' He gestured to the opposite end of the long table.

'I'll stand, if it's alright with you,' Mr Yule replied in the high-pitched timbre of the animal he resembled.

'Whatever you wish. Please begin when you're ready.'

Mr Yule shuffled round to the end of the board room table. He placed his bulging briefcase on the floor and spent the next few minutes transferring documents from the case to the table in front of him.

He reminded Gildchrist of a boy she'd known at the state secondary school she'd attended after her father went bankrupt. Belying his self-deprecating demeanour, this boy had bullied Gildchrist mercilessly. His way of welcoming the new girl had been to say, 'I hear your dad's a waster and your mum's a worthless piece of nonsense who couldn't get a job to save her life.' Over the years, he had tried to chip away at the young Gildchrist's confidence, undermining her at every opportunity. Gildchrist hadn't let it affect her, however. Instead she'd learned to develop a thick skin. Her ruthless streak came later, in fifth year, when she started inventing interesting ways to avenge her tormentors. She smiled at the thought.

'OK. I think we're ready now,' said Mr Yule. He straightened up and adjusted his spectacles. A light sheen of sweat made his forehead glow.

'Thank you for asking me to come and speak to you,' he said, looking at the expectant faces round the table. 'There has been a lot of speculation in the press recently about the weather front heading this way. Unfortunately, it's going to be much worse than the current predictions.'

There was a concerned murmur round the table.

Mr Yule continued. 'There will be thunderstorms and winds gusting up to 300 kilometres per hour. Remember the storm ten years ago, that spawned 1400 lightning strikes a minute and dumped 130mm of rain in an hour? Well, this storm is going to be several times worse than that. Instead of hail stones the size of golf balls, we will experience hail stones the size of baseballs. There will be flash floods throughout the city and twisters that can take the tops off buildings as easily as opening a bottle of pop. Our satellite images show that the storm is gathering force as it moves across land from the east coast. It is due to hit Macimanito in three days' time.'

Yule held up photographs of the devastation wreaked by some of the worst tornadoes in the country over the past twenty-five years, and started passing them round the table. There were mutterings from the committee members as they looked at the pictures and started discussing the implications of such a fierce storm.

Gildchrist tried not to show her pleasure looking at the scenes of destruction. Yes, yes, yes! She thought. This is exactly what I've been hoping for. The Mayor has neither the gumption nor the finances to rebuild the city. All the people will leave, and it will be mine!

'And how certain are we that this magnitude of storm will definitely hit our city within the next few days?' asked Mayor Klimpton.

'We've been tracking this one for some time, and we're as certain as we can be that the weather front is going to *capitalise?*

increase in intensity rather than decrease as it travels west. In short, it will reach its maximum strength when it hits Macimanito.'

There was silence as everyone absorbed the devastating news.

'Thank you, Mr Yule. Please keep us informed if there is any change in your forecast.'

Taking the hint, the meteorologist gathered his papers, shoved them into his briefcase and shuffled out of the room, nodding to the Mayor as he left.

The executive from Alba Oil spoke first. 'The Skyway needs to be working at one hundred percent efficiency if the city is to withstand this storm.'

'Indeed,' the Mayor nodded sagely. 'How close are we to finding the correct sequencing for the generators, Reggie?'

'As you know, there are several thousand possible combinations of four numbers between one and nine. Any one of these could be the correct sequence that Dr Lancing used in re-engineering the Skyway when it started to fail. We have been trying for nine years already and we haven't found it yet, despite advances in computational power. Only by activating the generators with the correct number of seconds between each can we maximise the electro-magnets' field and neutralise the natural forces under the city that channel the storms.'

'But you've managed to keep other storms at bay since we lost the code,' piped up another of the company executives.

'Any other sequence will produce a force field which goes some way to dampening the effect of the storms. But for a super storm like this, we need the full power of the Skyway to prevent a disaster.'

'What are you saying Reggie?' asked Gildchrist innocently.

She already knew the answer, but she wanted to hear him say it.

'Unless we hit upon the right code in the next few days, this city will be destroyed.'

The noise level in the room suddenly rose as everyone started talking at once.

'Quiet, quiet!' said the Mayor.

'And what are the chances of us finding the code?' he asked.

'As it happens, we may have a lead,' said Reggie. 'There's a young girl of Takoda ancestry whose father, coincidentally, worked on the geophysical survey of the city after the Skyway was built. She may be able to help us. Kitchi is liaising with her.'

Gildchrist smiled inwardly.

Oh no he isn't. I have her. She's mine.

'Excellent, excellent,' said the Mayor. 'I want an hourly report on developments, which I shall cascade to everyone around this table. If all else fails, we shall have to evacuate the city. Gentlemen … and lady,' he smiled at Gildchrist, 'may I remind you that everything discussed in these meetings is confidential. Please keep it that way. We don't want a panic on our hands.'

LOCKDOWN

Lizzie didn't stop beating her fists on her captor's back the entire time it took Gildchrist's gorillas to carry them below ground level, along a corridor and throw them into a windowless room. They had slammed the thick, steel door behind them with a resounding clang. A narrow slit the size of a letterbox at the base of the door was the only source of light in the room. It sent a dull yellow beam fanning out across the concrete floor. Both had been roughly dumped on to a padded bench against the wall opposite the door.

'How dare she! How dare she!' said Lizzie, still fuming. She sat with her back against the wall, her hands clasped around her knees. Her spectacles had managed to stay on for most of the ride. They'd fallen off as she was plonked on the bench. One lens had cracked. She stared into the skewed space in front of her, her mouth taut with anger.

Why didn't I listen to Josh? If I hadn't agreed to go with that man, we wouldn't be in this mess. Every action has an equal and opposite reaction. Right? Newton's Third Law of Motion. Gildchrist can't get away with this.

Lizzie felt tears of frustration start to form in her eyes. Josh said nothing. He lay curled up on the bench, his arms crossed against his chest, his knees tucked up in front of him.

Lizzie turned to her friend. 'Josh? Say something.'

Silence.

Lizzie's angry tone changed to one of concern. 'Josh. What's wrong with you?'

'C...c...can't talk. Teeth ch... ch... chattering too much.'

She inched closer to him. Leaning over, she peered into his face. His eyes were shut tight.

'I think you must be in shock. I read about it somewhere. Let's see if I can remember the symptoms. Are you feeling clammy?'

She touched the back of his hand.

'Urrgh! Yes, you are.'

'Unable to form words? - I think that's a yes. How about feeling dizzy?'

'Do sh...sh... shut up Lizzie! I think you're probably right. Can we talk less about what's just happened and more about how we're going to get out of here?'

Josh slowly uncurled his legs and arms and sat up straight. His pale face shone like a moon in the darkened room.

'The first thing we need to try and figure out is why that horrible woman wants to get into Dr Lancing's office. She's obviously up to no good.'

'Obviously,' muttered Josh.

'And she clearly wants it very badly, otherwise she wouldn't have locked us in here until we tell her the code to get in.'

'Or......' said Josh, finally coming to his senses. 'She put us in here under another, what-do-you-call-it?'

'Pretext.'

'Yes. Pretext. Maybe she just wants to keep us out of the way.'

'Why do you say that?' asked Lizzie.

'Well, think about it. You remember we heard her and that street guy arguing when we were waiting in Gildchrist's office? Maybe Toni, as she says she's called, was angry her man had brought us to her. After all, we now know the Gildchrist Corporation has something to do with the Skyway and its real purpose. Maybe we weren't supposed to know that. Toni was put on the spot, so her only option, in her warped mind, was to lock us up until she decides what to do next.'

'Or we cough up the code to get into Lancing's office,' Lizzie said.

'But you don't know the code, do you?' said Josh. 'Just the four numbers that make up the sequence.'

'That's right, but there are only twenty-four combinations of four, five, seven and eight so that's not many to try before she hits on the right one.'

'Either way, it doesn't look good for us. If you give her the numbers, she may decide we're no longer required and then, well....'

Lizzie and Josh fell silent. The seriousness of their situation suddenly dawned on them.

A deep 'clunk' broke the silence. The door swung open. A figure dressed in a white coat, his face in shadow, stood in the doorway. The two heavies were silhouetted in the background.

Everything happened so quickly, Lizzie and Josh had no time to react. In a few swift moves, the muscle men stepped forward, grabbed Lizzie and Josh's arms and bent them behind their backs, standing on their feet to stop them kicking out. The white-coated figure moved forward and stuck a hypodermic needle first in Lizzie's arm and then in Josh's, injecting a thick, colourless substance with one quick push of the plunger. Both instantly succumbed to the drug and slumped on-to the bench, fast asleep.

***

Toni Gildchrist paced the floor of her office like a caged tiger. The next few days played out in her mind - the girl would give her the sequencing code to maximise the Skyway's electro-magnetic field. She would enter it in reverse, doubling or even quadrupling the natural force field under the city. This would bring the epicentre of the impending storm right into the heart of Macimanito in double-quick time with devastating effect. The city would be erased from the face of the earth, and she would reap the reward of its hidden riches. There's no such thing as too much wealth, she reasoned, especially when your family's reputation is at stake. Wealth brought power and influence. All those people who had teased and criticised her over the years would eat their words when she ruled the country's diamond mining industry.

There was a gentle knock at the door. 'One of the watchers is here to see you, Madam,' said Clarissa, poking her head round the door.

Gildchrist snarled. 'Let him in, the little toe rag.'

'What on earth possessed you to bring them here, you idiot?' Gildchrist's rage was reignited at the sight of the watcher who visibly shrank at the verbal assault.

'I thought you wanted to know the code Sir, I mean Madam,' he said, squirming where he stood.

'Yes, yes, but bringing them here, to my office, to meet me .... You know what this means, don't you?'

'What's that Madam?'

'Well, now they know my involvement in the Skyway ... They can't leave here alive. And it will be you who has to despatch them to their untimely deaths.'

'But ... but ... why?' He was no killer and he certainly hadn't signed up for anything other than a bit of detective work.

'What do you mean why? Why do they have to die or why do you have to kill them?'

'Both!'

Gildchrist hadn't told either of her watchers about her plan to destroy the city. They had been employed on a 'need to know' basis and neither of them needed to know her real intentions.

'Oh, never mind,' she said with a sigh. 'Just make sure the girl tells us the code.'

Why do I always choose such lily-livered employees? she thought. I need unscrupulous individuals who will do my dirty work for me, discreetly and cleanly, leaving no trace. I can't have my public persona stained by scandal like my father's, not when I'm trying to rebuild the family fortune.

'Actually Madam, I have an idea how we can get her to talk,' said the watcher.

He paused for dramatic effect.

'Well, what is it man, what is it?' Gildchrist said impatiently.

'I think we can nobble the boy and get him to lean on the girl.'

'Are you speaking in tongues or something? Nobble? lean? - speak in plain English man.'

'We know they've both met Kitchi and there's a reasonable chance he has gained their trust. I can persuade the boy that Kitchi is working with us and wants them to co-operate. That Kitchi wants the girl to give you the code.'

'But why on earth would he believe you?'

'You know you asked me to find out as much as I could about the girl? Well, I found out her great-grandfather was a member of the Takoda First People's tribe, as is Kitchi. What's more, my colleague saw this drop out of Kitchi's pocket when he was following him.' He opened his palm and held it up to Gildchrist.

'What is it?' she asked, examining the object in the watcher's hand.

'It's a bone arrowhead. And the girl wears one just like it around her neck. This is what Kitchi would give someone to prove they are one of his trusted messengers.'

'Well, it's worth a try. If that fails, we shall have to use more traditional methods of getting them to talk.'

The watcher went ashen.

'Off you go then. There's no time to lose.' Gildchrist dismissed him with a wave of the hand.

Sounds like a hair-brained scheme to me, she thought. Might just work. It better had, for his sake.

***

A small, black, furry arm appeared sideways through the gap, pawing at the space. A whiskered face inched through, then quickly pulled back. This happened three or four times before two arms and a head finally emerged. The paws scrabbled frantically on the smooth floor, dragging with them the body, two legs and tail of the feline Houdini.

Josh had been observing Celeste's desperate entry through one half-open eye as he lay drowsily on the bench next to Lizzie. He opened his other eye and tried to sit up.

Still groggy from the sleeping draught administered eighteen hours earlier, he slid back down the wall on to the bench. He managed to stay upright on his second attempt, just as Celeste leaped on to his lap. She started kneading his legs with her sharp claws before curling up and starting to purr.

'Hello there,' he said quietly, smoothing her back. 'Come to visit us, have you?'

'Who are you talking to?' Lizzie mumbled, regaining consciousness as she lay flat out on the bench.

'It's the cat from the underground chamber.'

'Oh.' Lizzie's brain was too befuddled to wonder how the cat got in. 'What on earth did they give us?' she said, easing her way up into a sitting position.

'Whatever it was, it knocked us out. I wonder how long we've been asleep.'

At that moment, they heard the clunk of the door handle. Celeste jumped off Josh's lap and ran behind the door.

'Ah, I'm glad to see you've woken up,' said the scruffy man from the Skyway. He tried to sound cheery. 'I bet you're hungry. I've brought you something to eat. Got to keep our strength up, haven't we?'

He placed two red plastic trays on the bench beside Lizzie and Josh. The smell of beef burger and chips permeated the air. Josh could feel his mouth filling with saliva.

'How long have we been here,' asked Lizzie, subdued by the drugs, all fight gone from her.

'It's Monday. Monday afternoon,' he said. 'You've had a good, long sleep. Now it's time to eat. When you've finished, I'll be back for a bit of a chat. Let's see if we can get you out of here,' he said, backing out and locking the door behind him.

A MESSAGE

Josh savoured his last chip. He was licking the salt off his lips when the familiar sound of the door opening echoed off the walls of the cell.

'Was that good?' asked the watcher. He stood in the doorway looking at the empty trays. 'Right you are. A quick word, young sir.'

'What about Lizzie?' Josh protested. He didn't want to leave his friend.

'Yes, what about me?' Lizzie's spirit had returned as the drugs had worn off and the food had given her renewed energy.

'Don't worry, don't worry. I'll bring him back soon enough,' he said, trying to sound reassuring.

The door closed with a metallic squeal and a 'clunk'.

Fear took hold of Lizzie. *What if Josh doesn't come back? She* felt brave, invincible even with Josh by her side, but alone ... alone she felt vulnerable. She pushed back these negative thoughts. *Negative energy. Something to do with wormholes, allowing time travel.* If only she could harness her negative thoughts to get them out of here. *Wait a minute ...*

The cat.

Celeste had managed to evade detection. She jumped on the bench, stretched her front paws across Lizzie's lap and looked up into her face.

'How did you get in here? Was it through there?'

Lizzie pointed to the opening at the bottom of the door. *If you got in here through that narrow gap, you can get out of there as well.*

Her face lit up as she started to hatch a plan.

***

Reggie was looking agitated as the Control Pod door whooshed open and Kitchi entered. Mopping the beads of sweat from his brow with the sleeve of his overalls, he was leaning over the shoulder of one of his technicians. He pointed at the computer monitor in front of him.

'Have you heard?' Reggie turned to his friend. 'We have less than three days to figure out the correct sequencing of the electro-magnets or this city is finished. The storm to end all storms is heading our way. Where are we with the girl? How sure are you that she has the code?'

'I'm as sure as I can be,' he said.

'Darn it man, we have to be one hundred percent certain!' Reggie shouted, thumping his fist on the table. 'I'm sorry. I know you're behind us on this. It's just we have so little time and the chance we'll hit on the right sequence when we need it most is looking extremely remote. She is our last hope.'

Kitchi was silent for a moment.

' She is connected to this land. Her great-grandfather, a Takoda tribesman. Her own father, a Skyway geophysicist. The numbers she has are pre-ordained. It was she who came to the Skyway. She who found Dr Lancing's office …' The scarring on Kitchi's face burned a livid red as his voice took on a new intensity.

'Alright, alright man. I believe you. You've spoken to her and the boy?'

'I found them in one of the pods among the electro-magnet arrays.'

'Did she tell you the numbers?'

'No. Why would she? I think I might have …. scared them a little, unfortunately.' Kitchi instinctively touched his damaged face. 'I need to gain their trust before we get anything more out of her.'

'Well, what are you waiting for? Where are they now? Probably in school. Wait for them there. Walk them home, have a chat with them. Try and look less ... menacing ... Smile more. Do something!'

'That's just it, Reggie. Haven't you seen the news today? It seems that our two young friends - Lizzie Chambers and Josh Stapleton - have gone missing. They haven't been seen by their families since Saturday evening.'

'What! This is a disaster!' Reggie held his head in his hands. 'Where can they have gone? What are we going to do?'

'Stay calm, chief. We know where they were on Sunday. Something must have happened after I left them. I have a feeling I know who's behind their disappearance.'

Kitchi turned to go, leaving Reggie as agitated as when he had first arrived. As he approached the door, it automatically slid open and a tiny bundle of black fur on legs sauntered into the room.

'There you are!' said Kitchi. He bent down and picked up Celeste. She started rubbing her head against a button on his coat, purring softly.

As Kitchi moved his hand along the cat's silky head, he felt something on her neck. Parting the fur with his fingers, he found a piece of knotted string with a tube of paper wrapped round it. He gently placed Celeste back on the floor, undid the knot and opened the piece of paper. A message in shaky handwriting read:

Help! Locked up by woman called Toni.

Gildchrist building.

'Look at this,' he said, handing the paper to Reggie. 'As I suspected, Gildchrist has got them.'

'The witch! We know why she's holding them. She wants to get her hands on the code to sabotage the Skyway. We have to rescue them, and soon.'

'Leave it to me Reggie,' said Kitchi heading for the door.

THE TALISMAN

Lizzie took the object from Josh's palm.

'It's like the one Grandpa gave me,' she said. 'And this belongs to the white-haired man, to Kitchi?'

'That's what Toni's henchman just told me. He said Kitchi sent him with the talisman and a message for us. He wants us to co-operate with Toni,–Toni Gildchrist, the person who owns this company.'

'Grandpa told me this belonged to my great-grandfather who was from the Takoda tribe,' said Lizzie, lifting her necklace up to show Josh. 'They are very rare, precious tokens that are supposed to embody the spirit and supernatural powers of the animal from which they are made. The white-haired man - Kitchi – wouldn't have given this away lightly.

'You see these black markings on the bone?' she said, flipping over the loose arrowhead. 'These are made using a special tool and charcoal, which is then fused on to the surface by a method known only to the Takoda. Tokens like these cannot be faked.'

Holding a bone arrowhead in each hand she fell silent. Her brow became furrowed and her nose crinkled upwards. Doubt flooded her thoughts. Although she had been scared by the white-haired man initially, especially after she saw his face close, she had started to feel a connection with him - a deep, visceral connection. But was he friend or foe? She had to decide and quickly. At least it will get us out of here.

'OK. Let's do this,' she said.

'But ....' Josh started.

And then she remembered.

'On no ....' She said, feeling embarrassed.

I should have waited to talk to Josh before sending the cat out with a message. But I wasn't sure if he was coming back. I had to do something.

'What is it?' asked Josh.

'While you were out with the bearded guy, I tied a note asking for help round the neck of the cat. I reckoned she probably belonged to Kitchi as they seemed to know each other. I was kind of hoping the message would find its way to him.'

'So?'

'So ... I'm going to look a proper idiot now if Kitchi gets the message. He's going to wonder why we're asking for help when he's told us to play along with Toni.'

'That's assuming he did,' countered Josh. 'What happens if this is a trick to get you to tell Gildchrist your numbers?'

'I've thought of that,' said Lizzie, 'but this is a genuine Takoda talisman and my instinct tells me that Kitchi and Gildchrist know each other. You want to get out of here don't you?'

'Yes of course, but ...'

'No buts Josh. Let's go and see Toni.'

Lizzie hammered on the door and hollered 'Hey! Is anybody out there! We want to talk to Miss Gildchrist! Hey! Let us out!'

The cover of a small square hatch about two-thirds up the door slid open and two bulging brown eyes and a squashed nose appeared. 'What do you want?' one of the heavies said gruffly.

'We want to speak to Miss Gildchrist.'

'Wait.' He slammed shut the hatch cover. A few moments later Lizzie heard the handle being turned on the other side and the metallic squeal as the door opened. The two bald-headed special services men entered the room.

'Right, you two. No funny business. You're coming with us. My colleague here will lead the way and I will bring up the rear. Try anything and you'll be coming straight back in here. Understood?' The men looked menacing.

'Understood,' said Lizzie, imitating his deep, growly voice.

He looked at her with a piercing stare, then shoved her roughly out the door behind his companion. Josh followed. The four of them made their way along a narrow, concrete passageway, up several flights of stairs, into a service elevator and up more floors until they finally reached the reception area of Gildchrist's office. Stepping out of the elevator, the men frog-marched Lizzie and Josh into her office.

'Ah. Here we are again,' said Gildchrist. She motioned for the two young people to take a seat in front of her desk. The two gorillas took up their positions by the door.

'I understand you have had second thoughts about helping me out. You've decided to cough up the numbers that seem to have fortuitously landed in your lap.'

'They appeared in my birth chart actually,' said Lizzie haughtily. She didn't like this ice queen with her expensive dress sense and flashy ring.

'Indeed, indeed.' Toni smiled falsely as she tried to contain her impatience.

'How you came by them is not my concern. You used them to get into Lancing's office - correct?'

'Correct.'

'That's good enough for me. So, tell me my dear. What are they?'

'You first.'

'What do you mean you first?' Gildchrist was outraged at her impudence.

Yes, what does she mean 'you first'? thought Josh, who was feeling increasingly nervous at the way this exchange was going.

'You said you would tell us the secret of the Skyway if I told you the code for Lancing's office. So, I think it's only fair that you tell us the secret first and then I'll tell you what you want to know.'

Gildchrist could feel her blood pressure rising.

'How about we do it the other way around,' she said between gritted teeth.

Lizzie crossed her arms tightly and looked directly at her, lips pursed.

'You haven't been man-handled by two thugs, drugged and locked in a cell for the past twenty-four hours. You owe us missus.'

Lizzie's courage had returned. She felt the power of the two talismen, one round her neck, the other in her fist. Takoda magic surged through her body, energising her fighting spirit.

Gildchrist tried to stay composed by reminding herself that she would be rid of these pesky youngsters soon enough, once they had told her the code. Under the circumstances - their impending death - she decided there was no harm in giving them an edited version of why the Skyway had been built.

'You're right, of course,' she said in a conciliatory tone. 'You want to know the secret of the Skyway? OK ...' She clasped her hands under her chin, eyes closed, contemplating what to tell them.

'We already know about the magnets and what happens when they're activated,' Lizzie blurted out.

'Do you indeed? Then what more can I tell you?'

'The white-haired man... Kitchi ... didn't explain why they need to create an electro-magnetic field under the city. What's down there?'

'Ah, Kitchi, that meddling geophysicist. If only he'd managed to accidentally fall into one of his exploratory pits like the other one did,' she muttered under her breath.

'What did you say?' said Lizzie sharply. A disturbing thought surfaced.

'Oh nothing, nothing.' She waved the sentence away. 'The magnets are merely a ......'

BOOM!

The doors to Gildchrist's office flew open. Knocked off balance, the two heavies were pitched on to the floor. They lay there, arms sprawled out in front of them.

Kitchi burst into the room.

'Where are they?' he roared. His surprise at finding Lizzie and Josh sitting in front of him quickly turned to dismay.

'What did you tell her?' He looked at Lizzie, his face paling at the realisation that he might be too late.

'N ... nothing,' said Lizzie, confused.

'She hasn't told her anything yet,' Josh said, springing to Lizzie's defence. 'But didn't you tell us we should co-operate with Miss Gildchrist?'

'Never in a million years would I suggest you take that woman into your confidence,' he said, pointing at Gildchrist.

As Kitchi's words sank in, the two special service men regained their equilibrium and stood up, dusting themselves off. They quietly took positions behind Kitchi, ready to make a grab for him when Gildchrist gave them the word. Lizzie looked at Josh and gave an almost imperceptible nod. Kitchi saw it too. He turned to the man on his right.

THWACK!

One swift upper cut and he was felled.

THUMP!

Lizzie kicked the other man between the legs. He bent over in agony.

CRACK!

Josh smashed a glass paper weight over his head. Both men crumpled to the floor, watched by Gildchrist. Her lip curled in disgust at their feebleness.

'Quickly, let's get out of here,' said Kitchi. They headed for the door, pausing for a moment as Kitchi turned to look at Gildchrist. His dark eyes flashed with hatred at his nemesis.

'As for you, you gold-digger. Macimanito will never let you pillage the land she rests on. Not if I have anything to do with it.'

SAFE HOUSE

'Quickly, this way.' Kitchi led them out of Gildchrist's office and through the nearest fire exit. 'Those thugs will come to their senses soon. We need to get out of this building.'

They ran down countless concrete stairways, finally emerging at the lobby level. Scooting across the marble floor they pushed through the turnstiles and out on to the street. Nightfall was approaching. The tall buildings in their mantle of dusk seemed to lean forward, peering down on them like curious wraiths. The city was quiet and colourless. Only the silently changing traffic lights and occasional passing car disturbed the calm. No one saw the three figures dash into the nearest alleyway where they slowed their pace and started to wend their way across the city.

'Where are we going?' said Josh. He'd hardly spoken a word since the confrontation in Gildchrist's office.

'I'm taking you to Dr Lancing's old house. It's been empty for years. You'll be safe there for the next day or so.'

'But why can't we go home?' he said. His parents would be frantic.

'It's far too dangerous. Gildchrist knows where you live and will stop at nothing to capture you both again and try and extract the code. In a few days' time, it will all be over. You can return to your families then.'

'What will be over?' asked Lizzie.

'A massive storm is due to hit Macimanito in a couple of days' time. If we don't get the sequencing right to activate the electro-magnets, all will be lost. The city as we know it will no longer exist.'

A catastrophic natural event. That's what Grandpa saw in my birth chart. But how am I supposed to stop it?

'B ... B... But ...' said Josh.

'Lizzie has the number sequence we need to maximise the power of the magnets,' said Kitchi.

'But she has it, not me. Why can't you let me go?'

Lizzie was gutted. *Desert me now would you? After all we've been through!*

'Gildchrist will simply try and get to Lizzie through you. You both need to stay out of sight. I'm giving you twenty-four hours to think about what I've said.'

'Why should we trust you?' protested Lizzie. 'You said we should give Gildchrist the code. You gave one of her men your bone arrowhead to show us as proof the message came from you.' Lizzie put her hand in her pocket and brought out the talisman.

'Give that back to me,' he growled. 'Do you know how precious this is to me? Do you have any idea ...?'

'I do, actually,' said Lizzie. She was hurt and angry that he thought she'd taken it. 'I have one of my own. It belonged to my great-grandfather.' She lifted her necklace up to show him.

'That devil must have stolen it from me,' Kitchi muttered. 'Gildchrist has her own reasons for wanting the code for the arrays, and it's not to save the city, believe me.'

The three companions fell silent: Kitchi lost in his own thoughts, Lizzie and Josh trying to understand all that had happened to them in the past few days.

They headed west towards the setting sun. As the tall buildings gradually petered out, giving way to low-rise blocks and individual houses, the crimson vista expanded, filling the sky.

Kitchi's injured face, in shadow as they navigated the alleyways, came into view. Its rawness accentuated by the wounding light.

Lizzie was overcome with curiosity. She couldn't help herself from asking, 'What happened to your face?'

Josh gave her a filthy look.

'It was burned in a fire. Dr Lancing and three of his engineers died. I couldn't save them.'

Lizzie detected the sadness in his voice.

'It all happened a long time ago. A communication malfunction occurred between the control pod and the generators. There was something wrong with the transponders. He and his men were forced to manually input the code. Lightning hit directly above the generator room. The Skyway's earthing system had been breached. There was a massive explosion and a fire. I was in the communications tower and ran down, but I couldn't get near them.'

'Was he your friend?' asked Lizzie quietly.

'Yes; a dear, old friend and a brilliant mind. He built the magnetic array under the Skyway in the form of a pentagram to create a powerful magnetic field. When it started to fail, it was he who realised the magnets had to be activated in a certain order with specific time intervals between each to maximise the force field.

'There was always a danger, however, that the sequencing code, in the wrong hands, could be used to have the opposite effect and bring about the destruction of the city. That's why it was kept a secret by Dr Lancing. When he died, the code was lost. We have been trying for the last nine years, every combination of four numbers between one and nine to hit on the correct sequence. There are too many possible combinations and not enough time. We knew that one day a storm would hit us that was so ferocious only Dr Lancing's code could save us.'

'And the storm that's coming in a few days - that's the one?' asked Lizzie.

'That's the one. Now do you see why we need you to tell us the numbers? Your ancestors were Takoda, Lizzie. You are bound to this land and you have been sent these numbers for a reason. It is your destiny to save Macimanito and preserve the land it stands on.'

Lizzie pondered his words. Suddenly, she realised the enormous responsibility that had been placed on her shoulders. What had started out as an adventure now seemed more of a burden. She wasn't sure if she was up to the job.

What if I fail? What if my numbers are meaningless? I should have listened to Josh's reservations about my birth chart. There's nothing scientific about it at all. It's mystical nonsense. My mum was right. Why did I listen to Grandpa? If I fail, I'll be letting down not only everyone who lives in the city, but my family, my friends and even my ancestors.

'We're almost there,' said Kitchi. They walked another block, turned a corner, and there it was: An impressive stone-built house with doors boarded up, curtains drawn.

'Round the back,' instructed Kitchi. He looked up and down the street before leading them through a side gate into the garden. Pulling a large metal key from his pocket, he unlocked a small wooden door at the rear of the house. The door opened to reveal a steep staircase leading upwards.

'In you go,' he said, waving them through. 'You can leave the house at any time, but I suggest you don't. Gildchrist's men could be anywhere and we want to keep you safe until the time comes. Keep the curtains closed.'

Lizzie and Josh mounted the stairs. Looking back, they realised Kitchi wasn't following them.

'Where're you going?' said Josh.

'I'm going to get you something to eat and let your parents know you're both safe and well,' and with that he left, locking the door behind him.

MACIMANITO'S SECRET

Lizzie and Josh ascended the staircase. It opened out into a small kitchen. The fading daylight trickled in around the edges of the window blinds. They could just make out pots and pans hanging from a wooden rack suspended from the high ceiling. A dated-looking cooking range occupied an alcove to one side. Wall and floor units with dark wood doors skirted the rest of the room, a stainless-steel sink completing the picture of abandoned domesticity.

'It doesn't look as though it's been lived in for years,' said Josh. He swiped a thick layer of dust off the nearest surface. 'Let's look at the rest of the house.' He was feeling uncomfortable in the gloom and didn't want to wait until it was completely dark to explore their temporary safe house.

Lizzie led the way into what appeared to be a dining room with a large, domed skylight. A giant mahogany table stood at its centre surrounded by six matching chairs. On either side, a dresser and sideboard displayed an assortment of crockery and serving dishes. A doorway in one wall led through to the living room with its large bay-window. Long, draped curtains puddled on to the carpet. An old sofa and a couple of armchairs covered in cushions exuded the smell of neglect.

Further exploration of the house revealed an empty conservatory at the other side of the house. The tiled floor was stained with dark circles from plant pots which had long since been removed. Upstairs there were three bedrooms, including one in the octagonal turret that looked out over the street, and a bathroom.

Making their way back down the main staircase, Lizzie fished out her torch and turned it on to illuminate the darkening interior. They went back into the living room and Lizzie stretched out on the sofa. Josh sat in one of the armchairs, keeping his arms tucked in to avoid too much skin contact with the dusty upholstery.

'Well, there's nothing much of interest in here.' She was disappointed they'd found so few personal effects. She wanted to know more about the engineering genius Dr Lancing.

Maybe they're boxed somewhere in an attic or basement.

Against one wall, a bookcase leaned precariously into the room as if bowing to the visitors. 'Lend me your torch for a minute,' said Josh. He took the flashlight and scanned the titles on the shelves.

Lizzie thought about everything they'd learned over the last few days. The pieces of the puzzle were starting to fit into place. There were a few things that still didn't make sense though.

'Einstein's Theory of Special Relativity,' read Josh. 'The Experiments of Michael Faraday. Phffff – some heavy-duty books here. Look at the size of this one.' He lifted a tome from the bottom shelf. As he did so, the change in weight distribution unbalanced the bookcase, nudging it over its tipping point. It crashed on to the floor. Luckily, Josh's reaction time had been honed by years of dodging surprise attacks from aliens in video games. He managed to leap out of the way just in time.

'Whoa! That was close,' he said, feeling pleased with himself.

'For goodness sake Josh, stop wrecking the place. What's Kitchi going to say when he sees you've pulled the bookcase down?'

'I didn't. It fell by itself. All I did was take a book off the ....'

'Wait a minute!' said Lizzie, staring into the gloom. 'What's that?' She pointed at something behind Josh where the bookcase had stood.

He swung round with the torch, alarmed at what he might find.

'It's a door!' He tried turning the handle. 'And it's locked,' he said, deflated.

'And when has that ever stopped us?' said Lizzie, now standing close behind him. She pulled out a piece of metal bent at right-angles and her Swiss army knife. 'Watch and learn.' She inserted the first tool into the keyhole with her left hand. With the other, she wiggled the knife's detractable metal spike inside the lock. A few seconds later there was a 'click' and the door opened.

'Voila! We're in,' she said triumphantly.

Josh shone the torch through the doorway. A spiral metal staircase descended under the house.

'What do you think's down there?'

'Well there's only one way to find out,' said Lizzie. She took the torch from Josh's hand and started to descend. Josh followed, feeling his way in the semi-darkness.

At the bottom, Lizzie surveyed the room in the torchlight. On a shelf by the stairs she spotted a lantern and tried the switch. It worked. The room filled with a dull, yellowish light. Josh sighed with relief.

'Whoa!' he said, looking around him. A floor to ceiling wooden cabinet with a myriad of different-sized drawers occupied the whole of the back wall. To the left, pinned to the wall side by side were two, large aerial photos. To the right, a white board covered in writing and equations. Dominating the centre of the room, a huge desk piled high with maps and drawings.

One chart caught Josh's eye. Bright red concentric circles radiated out from the middle of the map, changing to blue then green. He went over to take a closer look. 'Ancient crater, Macimanito' it said in one corner.

'Hey, look at this, Lizzie,' he said, holding up the drawing. 'It's some sort of geological map. This must be where Kitchi and his team of geophysicists worked.'

My dad was one of them. If only he were here to tell us what's really going on.

She wandered over to the set of drawers. They were all labelled. The hand-written rectangles of paper in their metal holders were curled at the edges. She pulled open a drawer marked 'Core samples June 2003'. It was divided into six sections with a long tube of stone in each. She tried to lift one out.

'Umph, this is heavy.'

She stood cradling the sample in both hands. 'I wonder what it is?' She examined the layers of grey, white and black visible in the stone.

Josh went over to see.

'Looks like a sample of rock - probably from under the city. Didn't Kitchi say he and your dad were studying the geophysics of Macimanito?'

'There are lots of them from different dates.' Lizzie replaced the sample and started opening more of the drawers. In another one she found a handful of small, greenish-brown, black and grey pieces of stone. Holding them up to the light one by one she noticed that some of them were semi-transparent.

'This looks like glass.' She looked at the label on the drawer. 'But it says they're tektites.'

Josh wasn't listening. He was studying the two photos on one wall. 'You know what these are, don't you?' he said. 'They're aerial photographs of Macimanito. This one,' he pointed to the left-hand photo, 'was taken in the early 1940s. It says so in the title. See how few buildings there were then? Whereas this one,' he gestured to the right, 'is much more recent; it was taken in the 1990s. Do you notice something?'

Lizzie had joined him and was staring up at the photos.

'The escarpment around the city, which is clearly visible in both photographs, is almost a perfect circle,' said Josh.

'So?'

'Well, there aren't many naturally-occurring circular land formations, if any. Which can mean only one thing!'

Lizzie was growing impatient with the snail's pace of Josh's thought processes, but held her tongue. He's clearly on to something, or at least he thinks he is.

'The valley in which Macimanito sits must have been formed by a meteorite strike. Don't you remember Dr Galloway telling us how there've been at least thirty known meteorite strikes in this country over the last six hundred million years? He said that sometimes they are so big, nobody is aware of them until they show up on an aerial view of the land. Hang on a minute, what did you say was the name of those pieces of stone in that drawer?'

'Tektites.'

'That proves it! Tektites are globs of molten rock formed when a meteorite crashes to earth! I remember reading about them for our science class. It's all starting to make sense!' Josh clapped his hand to his forehead.

'What is?' Lizzie was frustrated that she hadn't paid more attention in that particular lesson.

'When a meteor hits earth, the impact heats up any iron in the underlying rock, making it more magnetic. That must have something to do with why there are electro-magnets under the Skyway.'

Before Lizzie or Josh had time to digest what they'd discovered, they heard footsteps above them.

'Uh oh! That must be Kitchi,' said Lizzie.

They quickly turned off the light and went back up the spiral stairway.

Kitchi had switched on a portable lamp in the corner of the room and did not look pleased when Lizzie and Josh emerged.

'I see you've found our office in the basement.'

'Well, it sort of found us,' said Lizzie. 'The book-shelves fell over and there it was!' She held her palms upwards and lifted her shoulders in an expression of surprise. She couldn't gauge their companion's mood and didn't want to rile him again.

'No matter,' he said. 'I would have shown you it anyway. Here, have some food and make yourselves comfortable for the night.' He placed a brown paper bag on a side table. The grease-stained carrier was printed with the name 'Alibaba Kabab'. Josh's nose twitched in anticipation.

'We know about the meteor strike and the magnetic field.' Lizzie couldn't help herself. Waiting until morning for answers was not an option.

'Do you indeed?' said Kitchi. 'Well there's a little more to it than meets the eye.'

'Are you going to tell us or what?' said Lizzie.

'Tomorrow. Now get some sleep. I'll be back in the morning.'

AN EXPLANATION

Uurgh!

Lizzie was frustrated with the pace of things. Kitchi had no sense of urgency. She wanted to know now! How was she ever going to save the city if she didn't understand what was going on?

She could tell Josh wasn't asleep. Stretched out on the sofa on top of his jacket, he was thinking. His eyes were closed but his breathing wasn't as regular as it should be if he was asleep.

'What's up?' she said.

'Nothing. Just mulling over what we found in the basement.'

'And?'

'There's something we're missing. Can't quite figure it out. I've been wracking my brains to remember something Dr Galloway said about a place in Africa that has been perplexing scientists because of its strong magnetic field.'

The hours passed. Neither of them slept. They were both relieved when they heard the back door open and saw Kitchi enter the room with breakfast.

'Here we are,' he said, handing the take-away bag to Josh. 'Sleep well?'

'No. I don't think I slept a wink.' Lizzie was grumpy.

'Nor me,' said Josh, a little more cheerfully. He started munching on a bacon and egg roll.

'We've got a long day ahead of us, so eat up and then splash some of this water on your faces to waken yourselves up.' He handed them a flask of water. 'I have news for you.'

'What news?'

'I went to see your mother and grandfather, Lizzie. Your mother remembers me from when I worked with your father. I told them you were alright and that you would be returned to them in a day or so. They were fearful for your safety. The mayor has ordered an evacuation of the city. I reassured them I would keep you safe.'

'Evacuation!' Lizzie and Josh both exclaimed.

Kitchi held up his hand to silence them. 'I'll explain later.'

'I advised your mother and grandfather to leave the area as soon as possible. They have gone to stay with your mother's sister in Idona.'

'But why?' Lizzie interjected.

'As I said, let me finish and then everything will become clear.' A note of irritation entered Kitchi's voice.

'Unfortunately,' he said, turning to Josh, 'I didn't reach your family in time. When I went to your house there was no-one at home. A concerned neighbour came out to tell me he had seen a black van pull up a few hours earlier. Two large bald men got out, barged into the house, dragged out your parents and brother, bundled them into the van and drove off.'

'What!' Bits of breakfast roll sprayed out of Josh's mouth.

'Gildchrist's men. She's obviously planning to use them to try and get Lizzie to tell her the code.'

Josh jumped up from his seat, a look of panic on his face.

'We've got to do something! What are we waiting for?'

'She's probably calling our bluff.' Kitchi tried to reassure Josh. 'I can't believe she wants the murder of three innocent people on her hands when Gildchrist

Corporation becomes one of the biggest diamond mining companies in the world.'

'Murder!' cried Josh.

'Diamonds!' said Lizzie.

'Yes, diamonds. I assume you've worked out that this city of ours is located in the crater of a meteor strike from millions of years ago? And that because of that strike there is a huge magnetic anomaly under the city.'

'Magnetic anomaly! That's what I was trying to remember from Dr Galloway's lesson,' said Josh.

'What's that?' asked Lizzie.

'It means there is a major disturbance in the earth's naturally-occurring magnetic field in the rocks under Macimanito. We carried out airborne and ground measurements of the magnetic field in this area as part of our geophysical survey before and after the Skyway was built. To determine the strength of force field required to neutralise the anomaly.'

'But why did you need to do that? What harm could the magnetic field do?' said Lizzie.

'During our investigations, we noticed that when there was a change in atmospheric pressure, with an approaching storm, the magnetic field under Macimanito strengthened significantly. It attracted the weather front. The magnetic forces then infused the storm clouds with electrical charge, making them far more destructive.'

'Wait a minute. Is that why the First People have a myth about a demon lying beneath the streets of the city?'

'Of course. Without the scientific know-how we have today, they came up with an explanation rooted in their cultural and sacred beliefs. A story that could be passed down through the generations and keep them safely away from this place.'

Lizzie crinkled her nose and closed her eyes.

Maybe the First People's stories aren't nonsense after all. I never thought there might be some truth in them.

'What about the diamonds?'

'When a meteorite hits the earth, molten debris called tektites are formed,' said Kitchi.

Josh looked at Lizzie and nodded.

'The pressure exerted on the earth in a meteorite strike can also create something a lot more precious than mere glass - diamonds. We found evidence of diamonds in the core samples we took in the late 1980s when Gildchrist came on the scene. She had been carrying out some of her own geological surveys. Her findings showed that Macimanito is sitting on huge diamond reserves. She applied for a licence to do some exploratory work but was blocked by the Mayor. He had spent millions of dollars of taxpayers' money building a new city and was not going to turn it into one big diamond mine.'

'So why does Gildchrist want the code?' asked Lizzie. She was still a little puzzled.

'She believes that reversing the activation sequence of the electro-magnets will turn the force field skyward, strengthening the forces coming up through the earth. When the approaching storm hits it will obliterate the city completely.'

'Wouldn't that please the Takoda? They would be able to reclaim the land.'

'Have you ever seen a diamond mine?' said Kitchi.

Silence.

'They're like gigantic holes in the earth. Some are deeper than 500m. The land is completely destroyed. The mining company blasts massive chunks out of the earth to get to the diamonds. The Takoda would rather have a city sitting on top of this land than have it gouged out and pillaged by a greedy corporation.

'So - are you willing to help us and save the city, or would you rather watch it burn and see Gildchrist plunder the land to become one of the richest women on the planet?'

'What do you think?' said Lizzie, jumping up from her seat. 'Let's do this!'

EVACUATION

Lizzie, Josh and Kitchi stepped out of Dr Lancing's house. Vehicles crowded the road. Anxious faces peered out from inside.

'What's happening?' said Lizzie.

'Everyone's leaving,' said Kitchi. 'The Mayor's not taking any chances.'

The people of Macimanito were on the move. Within half an hour of the evacuation order, the traffic started to build. Hundreds of cars, trucks and buses crawled through the city streets, picking up speed as they left the valley for the relative safety of the outlying plains to the south. Those who had been slow to heed the Mayor's warning hurriedly left their homes. Mothers and fathers bundled children, dogs and cats into cars. The elderly were helped into buses or relatives' vehicles. Disbelieving young couples, surprised by the exodus, changed their minds about staying and joined the throng.

'Keep moving and be patient!' Peace officers lining the roads every few hundred metres yelled instructions through loudhailers. 'If you break down, honk your horn and a tow truck will come and get you!'

Everyone looked up at the sky before boarding their vehicles. The children sensed their parents' panic but were otherwise unaware of the danger. The familiar signs of an approaching storm were there but this time something was different. Instead of the ominous bank of dark cloud which usually rolled in and hovered over the city before a thunderstorm, bulging columns of thick white cloud had started to form in the sky. An eerie silence fell over the city and an almost palpable crackle of electrically charged particles filled the air.

As the three figures quickly walked towards the city's downtown area, they heard shouts from passing cars.

'Hey, don't you know there's a storm coming?'

'Get your kids out of the city. We have to evacuate!'

'What are you doing? Didn't you hear the news this morning?'

They ignored the remarks and increased their pace as a light rain began to fall. The sky turned a strange purplish hue. They heard the distant rumble of thunder.

'It's starting,' said Kitchi. 'We need to hurry.'

He led them into the nearest stairwell to the Skyway and up along the yellow route heading east. Ten minutes later they reached the entrance to Electrix Towers. Kitchi pushed open the double glass doors. They entered the reception area of the building, where one security guard remained. Recognising Kitchi, he let them through to a bank of elevators. Kitchi hastily pushed the 'up' button and one set of doors opened.

'Why are we here?' asked Lizzie when they were in the elevator.

'You'll see,' said Kitchi.

They stepped out on to the fourteenth floor and entered a door marked 'Board Room'.

Mayor Klimpton and a group of suited men were sat round the board room table. Toni Gildchrist was notable by her absence. They fell silent when Kitchi entered with Lizzie and Josh.

'This is the girl I was telling you about,' said Reggie Grant, gesturing in Lizzie's direction.

Neither Lizzie nor Josh moved from their place beside Kitchi. Both were overawed by the presence of so many important-looking men with serious expressions.

'Do have a seat,' said the Mayor warmly. He realised the young people might feel intimidated by the company.

Chairs were pulled out for them on one side of the table and they took their places in silence.

'I understand you might be able to help us out, young lady,' he said to Lizzie.

'Who are you?' Lizzie replied suspiciously. She wasn't going to give anything away to this stranger.

'I can understand your caution, given the way you've been treated at the hands of one of our committee members.' He looked at the empty chair where Gildchrist should have been sitting. 'But I can assure you that was simply a misunderstanding.'

'So, Ms Gildchrist works with you?'

'Not exactly. We are all members of the Skyway Committee with the city's best interests at heart.'

'But I thought Ms Gildchrist ...'

'Never mind Gildchrist.' Kitchi stopped her before she could continue, 'She's not here now Lizzie. These gentlemen are our friends. Reggie here,' he looked at his colleague, 'is the chief engineer of the Skyway. He and his team have been working on the sequencing code.'

'I'd be happy to help you, Reggie,' said Lizzie, 'and Kitchi of course, but I won't be working with the rest of you.'

Mayor Klimpton blustered a response from the end of the table, which thankfully neither Lizzie nor Josh heard.

'That's fine,' said Reggie, keen to smooth things over with the rest of the committee. He was anxious to leave the meeting and get back to the Control Pod.

'My technicians are already trying different activation sequences for the electro-magnets and monitoring the changes in the magnetic field. When will the evacuation of the city be complete, Mayor Klimpton?'

'Everybody apart from essential personnel should have left by six o'clock this evening,' he said.

'And what's the latest on the approaching weather front?'

'Our meteorological office says it is due to hit between midnight tonight and four o'clock tomorrow morning.'

'That gives us about twelve hours at most to stop it. That's not long, Mayor. If you don't mind, I think we need to get back to work.' Reggie rose from his seat and motioned to Kitchi who did likewise, along with Lizzie and Josh.

The four of them started to leave the room.

'Of course,' Mayor Klimpton said to their retreating backs. 'We're counting on you!'

Kitchi and Reggie led the way, heading towards the Skyway entrance.

'Aren't we forgetting something?' said Josh, pulling on Kitchi's arm to slow him down.

'What's that?' He was preoccupied with the impending storm.

'Gildchrist has my family! If Lizzie gives you the code what will happen to them?'

'What!' said Reggie, turning to Kitchi. 'You never said...'

'I didn't have the chance,' said Kitchi. 'Gildchrist will do everything she can to stop Lizzie giving us the code. This is her latest ploy - threatening Josh's family.'

'And Lizzie's family?'

'They're safe. I made sure of that.'

'Good. We'll deal with Gildchrist when the time comes.'

THE CODE

Wending their way through the network of corridors, the four figures eventually arrived at a crossway. Kitchi flipped up the fire alarm box on one wall of the landing and punched in some numbers. A door slid open and they entered the elevator. A few minutes later and forty floors higher, they stepped out into the Control Pod.

'Wow!' said Lizzie. She looked at the row of monitors mounted high on the walls and the technicians busily working at computer terminals around the room.

'Where are we?'

'This, young lady,' said Reggie proudly, 'is the nerve centre of the Skyway. You see those monitors?' He pointed to the screens on the wall. 'The ones to the right are showing up-to-date information on the approaching weather front. They include satellite images and live visuals from neighbouring areas so we can monitor the progress of the storm. The screens to the left show digital replicas of the dials on the generators. We can see at a glance the size of the current passing through the array of electro-magnets. The monitors in the centre show live CCTV footage of the interior of the underground chambers and the car park entrance to the array complex.'

'And the electro-magnets have already been activated?' asked Lizzie.

'Yes. If we turn the sound on one of the centre screens,' Reggie nodded to one of his technicians who tapped on his keyboard, 'you can hear they are now live.'

A soft humming sound came from one of the monitors above them. Lizzie looked up at the screen. She wondered how such a gentle sound could be produced by such a mighty machine.

Electro-magnetic waves, those engineered by man and those produced by nature. Competing against each other, the one trying to cancel out the other.

Josh's attention was elsewhere. He was looking at the live camera footage from Claytown, 100km to the east of Macimanito. A thin finger of grey was starting to push out towards the earth from an angry mass of cloud. As he watched, another and then another started to form, like witches' fingers throwing down curses on the land.

'L ... look.' He pointed at the monitor.

'Yes, it's a big one. The biggest we've ever seen. What you're looking at now is a T1 with winds up to 90km an hour,' explained Reggie. 'Those ribbons of cloud are the beginnings of tornadoes. The storm's picking up speed and intensity as it travels west. By the time it reaches us it's expected to reach a T11, unless....'

'Unless we stop it,' said Kitchi. 'It picks up strength when it comes within about 10km of the city. The pull from the magnetic anomaly under Macimanito draws the weather system into the crater. We've only been able to reduce the magnetic field so far, not neutralise it. This storm is so big that weakening the pull from under the city is not enough. The tornado will gobble us up.'

'So, you've already tried some combinations of four numbers to sequence the generators, is that right?' asked Lizzie.

Reggie laughed. 'We've been trying for years. We have about a one in nine thousandth chance of hitting on the correct sequence and we haven't found it yet. You are our only hope.'

Lizzie hesitated. She felt her courage diminishing again. How could she tell them she knew the four numbers, but not the order they're supposed to go in? And then there was Josh's family to think about. If she revealed the numbers, she would be endangering their lives.

Her train of thought was interrupted by Kitchi.

'Look, it's Gildchrist.' He pointed to one of the CCTV screens.

'Mum, Dad, Dan!' Josh cried.

Gildchrist was in one of the chambers containing the electro-magnets. Her security men had handcuffed all three members of Josh's family to a metal loop attached to one of the large, yellow, humming machines. She looked up at the camera and started speaking. The sound had been left on.

'It was no idle threat, you see.' She gestured to Josh's struggling family members. Their mouths had been taped so they couldn't cry out. 'Unless the girl tells me the code, they will die. All I have to do is say the word and my men will kill the boy's family right here. You'd enjoy that, wouldn't you boys?' The gorillas grunted. 'So, we need to talk, yes? My place or yours? Oh, I forgot this camera only transmits sound one way. I guess it'll have to be your place then. Perhaps you can send your man out to meet me. And don't think you'll be able to rescue these poor souls.' She looked at Josh's family. 'Even if you do get past my security guards the handcuffs are made of titanium alloy.

You'd need more than a blow torch to get through all six bracelets and I'm afraid you simply don't have the time.' She smiled and then disappeared towards the chamber's exit.

'We have no time to lose Lizzie,' said Reggie. 'You must tell us the code immediately.'

Lizzie felt awkward. Her face started to colour.

'The numbers are four, five, eight and seven but ... but I can't remember the order they go in.'

'What!' boomed Reggie, turning to Kitchi. 'I thought you said she had the code?'

'She does, Reggie. Be patient. Think, Lizzie, think.' Kitchi tried to calm the situation. 'Close your eyes and go back a few days when you and Josh found Dr Lancing's office. Tell us exactly what happened.'

Lizzie closed her eyes. Her hand instinctively went around the bone arrowhead resting on her neck. 'Well ... there was a cabinet with glass sea creatures inside. They were of different colours and very beautiful. I wanted to touch them so much and my hand went through the glass wall of the cabinet as if it wasn't there.'

Reggie looked at Kitchi and was about to say something, but Kitchi lifted a hand to silence him. With the other he held on to the talisman now safely back in his pocket.

'I was quite surprised, but I tried again and the same thing happened. When I started to touch the creatures, I noticed they had nodules on their backs. There were four glass sculptures, each with different numbers of raised bumps. First I touched the ....' Lizzie tried hard to remember...'jellyfish I think, which had ...' she played through the scene in her mind 'seven nodules ... then the sea urchin, with ... four nodules ... the lilac box fish was next with more .... five bumps on its back and then the squid with ...' She ran her fingers through the air across the imaginary back of the glass creature 'eight.'

She opened her eyes. 'Seven, four, five, eight - that's the sequence!'

Reggie almost clapped his hands with joy. He was about to instruct his technicians to shut off the generators and reactivate the electro-magnets using the code, when Kitchi stopped him.

'Wait, my friend. We need to deal with Gildchrist first. She must not know that we have the code, otherwise three people's lives will be in danger.'

'Yes, that's my family we're talking about.' Josh was close to tears. Lizzie went to take his arm, but he shrugged her away. 'She's given you the code now. All you care about is saving the city. You don't care what happens to my family.'

'That's not true,' said Kitchi. He tried to sound reassuring. 'We will meet with Gildchrist and try and negotiate their release, somehow. There she is now.'

THE RESCUE

There was a buzzing sound and Gildchrist's face appeared on one of the screens.

'She's in the underground car park. I'll go and get her,' said Kitchi.

'Wait one second,' said Reggie. 'I have an idea. Susan, freeze that video on the lad's parents with those heavies standing next to them.'

'Yes, boss,' replied one of the technicians. She immediately typed the command into her workstation.

'Mike?'

'Yes chief?' said another technician.

Reggie pulled a seven-inch long cylinder from a yellow mesh holder attached to his waistband.

'Take my bear spray and your special tools.' He winked at Mike. 'Enter the chamber via the Skyway entrance. You know what to do. Oh, and take Celeste with you.' He scooped up the cat from his desk where she'd been napping next to his warm computer terminal. 'You never know when her talents might come in useful.'

'A bear spray?' said Josh, incredulous.

'Yes. For getting out of a tight spot with a grizzly or black bear when you're out hiking in the mountains. I keep it with me at all times, just in case.'

'But why? ....'

'There are two bear-sized men guarding your parents, son. What do you think it's for?'

'Oh!' Josh smiled. He turned to Lizzie. She was sitting on a desk, her chin resting on one clenched fist, her eyes shut, deep in thought.

'What's up Lizzie?' he asked, but she didn't hear him. She was concentrating hard trying to remember something.

'Right. Am I OK to go?' Kitchi asked.

'Yes - all set,' said Reggie. Mike headed for the exit, cradling Celeste.

Kitchi and Mike travelled together in the elevator to the Skyway, then they went their separate ways. Kitchi ran to the nearest elevator that would take him to the underground car park. When the doors slid open there was Gildchrist, languishing against a concrete pillar.

'There you are!' she sneered. 'What took you so long? Having trouble breathing?'

Kitchi ignored the jibe. The fire which had burned his face and hand had also scorched his lungs. Only a rigorous exercise regime had helped restore Kitchi's body to fitness.

'Well, are you coming or not?' he stepped back to allow Gildchrist to enter the elevator.

Gildchrist was afraid of Kitchi but she dared not show it. She remembered stories her father had told her, relayed by his grandfather, of the ferocity of the First People retaliating against attacks by white men during the Gold Rush. Now with his horribly scarred face, Kitchi looked twice as menacing. Gildchrist felt the adrenalin coursing through her body brought on by a mixture of fear and exhilaration. I'm so close, she thought, so close to fulfilling my heart's desire.

Stepping out into the Skyway, Kitchi took Gildchrist on an alternative route to the Control Pod avoiding the secret entrance he used. When the door to the tower room finally swished open, the relative calm of half an hour before had been replaced by frantic activity, bordering on panic.

Reggie was dashing from terminal to terminal, giving instructions to technicians. Lizzie and Josh were standing transfixed by the changing storm pictures on the monitors high up on the wall.

The sky visible through the windows had taken on an unearthly colour. Crashes of thunder and lightning flashes pummelled the tower. A bruised yellow and black bank of cloud hovered over Macimanito like a gigantic spaceship waiting to beam up the city-or sink down on top of it, crushing it into the ground.

A swirling vortex of wind tore branches off trees, knocked over pavement advertising boards and sucked up the contents of rubbish bins. Debris danced in the air until it was caught up in the moving maelstrom and hurled against the nearest building. Large gobbets of horizontal rain lashed against the sides of buildings.

The control tower seemed to audibly groan under the strain of the strengthening wind. The storm bombarded it with high voltage lightning strikes. It seemed intent on tearing it off its foundations like an enormous tuber out of the earth.

'My, my,' said Gildchrist. Hands clasped together under her chin, clearly delighted by the scene unfolding in front of her. Reggie, Lizzie and Josh turned to look at her.

'So, she hasn't spilled the beans yet?' She looked at Lizzie. 'Clever girl. You don't want your little friend's family to get hurt, do you?' She pouted.

'Less of the little, you moron!' Josh stepped towards her, snarling.

'Now, don't get upset. This won't take long. Now, my child. The code, if you please.' She smiled at Lizzie.

'What guarantee do I have that you'll let Josh's family go if I give you the sequence?'

'You have my word, of course. You can see they are still safe and well.' She gestured to the monitor showing Josh's mum, dad and brother. 'As soon as you give me the code, I will send my men a message to set them free. How about that?'

'Let them go first,' Lizzie countered.

'The time for silly games is over, my child. I'm outnumbered here.' She looked back at Kitchi and then at Reggie and his technicians. 'What guarantee do I have that once I let them go you will give me the code?'

'You have my word,' said Lizzie.

'Well that's all very well, but what about your friends here? They might have other ideas.'

'Looks like we have a stalemate,' growled Kitchi, placing one large hand on Gildchrist's shoulder.

Gildchrist decided to try a different tactic. 'Lizzie, you and I are so alike, if only you knew it. We have both lost our fathers and want to honour their memories in some way. If we work together, we can achieve both our goals at the same time.'

'How dare you mention Charles Chambers in the same breath as your father!' said Kitchi. 'Charles was ~~an~~ honourable ~~man~~, a scientist, a brilliant man. Your father was a ... a .... blaggard, a good-for-nothing. Look how you turned out!'

Gildchrist ignored Kitchi's outburst. She could see the uncertainty on Lizzie's face.

'Allowing this vicious storm to raze Macimanito to the ground will allow me to bring wealth and prosperity to this land and to your family. I am quite willing to negotiate a generous fee for your services, enough to keep you, your mother and grandfather comfortable for the rest of your lives.'

Lizzie looked from Gildchrist to Kitchi and back again. *Maybe she's right. Is this what my father would have wanted me to do? Instead of saving the city, I should be thinking of my family and their needs.*

Kitchi could sense her doubts.

'Don't listen to her, Lizzie. She's using you. Think of the lives devastated if the city is destroyed. Do you honestly believe that is what your mother and grandfather would want? The numbers were given to you, and you alone for a reason, for something bigger than personal gain. Follow your instinct Lizzie, follow your instinct.'

Lizzie closed her eyes tight and squeezed the talisman round her neck.

Tell me what to do. Please!

***

In the underground chamber Josh's parents had fallen silent, exhausted with trying to scream through the electrician's tape that covered their mouths. The handcuffs had started to cut into their wrists, leaving painful red welts. Dan, terrified by his ordeal, was whimpering softly. The heat from the electro-magnets was making them drowsy.

Gildchrist's men had also been feeling the heat in their long, leather coats. They had both fallen asleep, sitting with their backs up against the wall. Their bald heads had slipped sideways and come to rest against each other like two, shiny, flesh-coloured bowling balls. A muffled snore emanated from the mouth of one of them, complementing the low 'humm' of the electro-magnets.

Even if they had been awake it is doubtful either would have noticed the small, black, furry intruder who stealthily ran into the chamber and took up position on a ledge above their heads. Mike, who had been following Celeste, keeping close to the wall of the dark corridor to avoid being seen, was relieved when he saw that both men were asleep. Entering the chamber, he made eye contact with all three captives and put a finger to his lips. He positioned himself three feet in front of Gildchrist's heavies and quietly removed the canister of bear spray from his pocket, all the time looking at Celeste to make sure he had her attention. Taking off the safety catch from the can, he pointed an index finger at Celeste and then quickly swept it downwards towards the men.

Celeste leaped off her perch, all four paws stretched out, claws extended. As soon as she landed on their slippery pates she instinctively gripped as hard as she could, penetrating their scalps with her sharp talons, before bouncing off on to the floor. The effect was instantaneous. Both men opened their eyes and their mouths wide. An easy target for Mike, who sprayed the stinging pepper spray at them as fast and hard as he could.

Gildchrist's men leaped up, screaming. Their hands covered their eyes, their mouths starting to salivate. Mike spun each one round in turn and pushed them along the corridor. They stumbled forward, temporarily blinded and disorientated.

'Right, let's get you out of here,' he said, turning to Josh's parents. He gently removed the tape from each of their mouths and set to work picking the lock on Dan's handcuffs. One by one, he unlocked each set of cuffs. Dan ran to his mother. She picked him up and held him in her arms.

'Follow me,' said Mike. 'We have no time to lose. Those bruisers will raise the alarm soon.'

'But ...' said Josh's dad.

'There'll be time enough for questions when this is over. We need to leave now.'

He led them down a corridor in the opposite direction to their captors, up a stairwell and into the car park.

'Here, take Reggie's truck.' He handed Josh's dad some car keys and pointed to a bright red pick-up truck that stood in one of the spaces. 'Get out of town as fast as you can. Everyone has been evacuated to Leybridge in the south. Wait there.'

'But what about Josh?' his dad said.

'Josh is with us and he's fine. Now go!'

Josh's family, shaken but otherwise unharmed, did as they were asked. Mike watched them drive away and made his way back to the control tower.

***

Reggie turned as the door whooshed open and Mike entered, nodding to his boss.

'Let's see how Josh's family are doing, shall we?' He walked over to Susan and lightly tapped her shoulder.

Gildchrist looked puzzled. 'But we can see ...' At that moment, the monitor flickered and went live again. Gildchrist's heavies stumbled about the otherwise unoccupied pod, shouting profanities and rubbing their eyes. They kept bumping into each other and the electro-magnets.

'What the ...!'

Seizing the moment, Kitchi, who had been standing behind Gildchrist, grabbed her arms and pulled them tightly behind her back. Reggie sprang to his assistance, whipping some cable ties out of his tool pouch and securing them round Gildchrist's wrists. Together they pulled her down on to a chair.

'Lizzie!' she cried out. 'Are you with me or with them?'

She glared at her. 'Kitchi was right,' she said. 'You're no better than your father. You're a horrible woman who locks people up and threatens their families. Greed is what drives you and greed will be your undoing. I'm not helping you, not in a million years.'

Reggie quickly covered Gildchrist's mouth to silence her angry outbursts and tied her ankles together with more cable ties. A piece of old oil cloth served as a blindfold and ear cans were looped over her head, so she couldn't see or hear what was going on.

'Right - let's get down to business,' said Reggie, clapping his hands.

STORM CRITICAL

Dealing with Gildchrist had lost Reggie and his team precious time. The storm outside was gathering momentum, energised by the magnetic force field beneath the city, fuelled by street furniture, trees and cars. The swirling vortex of the giant tornado moved towards the control tower at the heart of the city. The monitors indicated a wind speed of 260km per hour. Much faster, and the skyscrapers would start to twist and buckle under the pressure. Their steel frames would be unable to withstand the enormous forces exerted by the rotating monster.

Reggie shouted instructions to his technicians.

'A and B stations stand-by to deactivate the magnets.'

'Susan, you have the code? As soon as the magnets are deactivated, key in the sequence.'

'C station. Keep an eye on any changes in Macimanito's force field.'

'Mike. It's your job to watch the meteorological data. The storm should dissipate once the electro-magnets are re-energised.'

'D station, don't take your eyes off those dials on the electro-magnets.'

'Are we all ready?'

'Yes, chief,' the technicians shouted in unison.

'Let's do this!' He started to count down with his fingers held high in the air. 'Five, four, three, two, one - de-activate NOW!'

The technicians nearest to him rapidly keyed in commands. One by one, the humming electro-magnets fell silent.

Susan had been waiting for the signal from Reggie. As soon as he nodded at her she carefully entered the time sequence to start up the five generators – seven, four, five, eight - and pressed a button to initiate the sequence.

There was absolute silence in the control room. Everyone listened for the sound of the electro-magnets buzzing back to life.

'How are we doing D station?'

'Building steadily boss; the electro-magnets are reaching their full strength .... now!'

Everyone held their breath.

A moment later, the ear-splitting sound of alarms filled the room. Red warning lights flashed above the monitors.

'It hasn't worked! It hasn't worked,' screamed Reggie, clutching his hair with both hands.

'The tornado is growing,' said one of the technicians. 'Winds are now 300km per hour. The city can't take much more, chief!'

A metallic roof covering slammed against the windows of the control tower, which continued to creak and groan under the onslaught. Above the noise of the alarms, what there was a sound sounded like an approaching freight train. The deadly vortex was now almost black in colour. As it spun towards the tower, forks of lightning crackled out from its core like the fiery tongues of dragons. Giant hailstones clattered on to the roof of the tower.

Lizzie, sitting in one corner of the room, covered her ears and scrunched her eyes closed. She couldn't stand it any longer.

Why did I believe Grandpa? Why did I convince myself and everyone else that I could save the city? Aargh!!

She could feel the pressure building in her head as the sight and sounds of the storm intensified. She sat on the floor, bringing up her knees and burying her head in her arms.

'Lizzie' said a quiet voice. 'Lizzie.' She felt an arm round her shoulder. Peering sideways she saw Josh's eyes looking into hers. 'I have an idea.' Instead of interrupting him or dismissing what he had to say before he could speak a word, she remained silent, listening.

'Remember telling me your grandpa read your numbers from your birth chart? Well maybe that's the correct sequence, the order in which he read them out.'

Lizzie sat up straight, wrinkled her nose and tried to remember. She recited her grandpa's words: '"Thirteen first, then eight, seven and lastly five". He gave me the sequence, but I didn't realise it at the time. It has to be right.' She looked up at Reggie.

'You need to try four, eight, seven, five.'

'Let's hope you're right. This is our last chance,' said Reggie. 'Right, get ready to shut down and start the activation again.' His voice belied the feeling of rising panic in his chest.

There was no countdown this time. The urgency of the situation was clear to everyone. The technicians followed the same steps they had carried out only minutes earlier, this time using the new number sequence.

Lizzie clutched her knees to her chest, head lowered, eyes shut. She couldn't bear it if she was wrong again. If the city was destroyed, it would be her fault and her fault alone. She'd had the code all along but had been too distracted to realise it.

Josh looped an arm around her shoulders once more and leaned in towards her. 'It'll work this time, just you watch,' he said quietly. 'You couldn't have done more than you have. You can't blame yourself for what would have been a natural disaster.'

'But I should have known sooner.' Lizzie was close to tears. 'I'm so disappointed with myself.'

Josh gave her a reassuring squeeze. 'Well, don't be. You're very special. A little impetuous at times ... ' Lizzie looked up and gave him a little punch on the arm. 'But a true go-getter. A proper little action woman.'

Throughout the activity in the Control Pod, Kitchi had maintained in stoic silence, standing guard beside Gildchrist, who had finally given up struggling. She sat motionless, her head hanging down in defeat.

Hope and anticipation hung in the air as the electromagnets were brought to life for a second time. Everyone waited. The seconds ticked by.

Mike was the first to speak. 'The wind speed is dropping Sir, and the tornado appears to be moving away.'

Reggie looked up at the windows and watched as the whirling monster seemed to shrink into itself. Reducing in size and ferocity, it changed direction, heading back east towards the prairies.

'And Macimanito's force field?' he asked.

'Neutralised chief.'

A TOKEN

POP!

The Champagne cork pinged against one of the cut-glass drops of the chandelier in Mayor Klimpton's dining room.

'Whoops! That was a close one.' He poured the bubbly drink into the glasses lined up on the huge oak dining table. When they were full, he started handing them out to the gathered throng. At the other end of the table, Mrs Klimpton poured soda into a smaller array of tumblers. She handed them to Lizzie, Josh and Dan.

'Let us all raise a glass,' began the Mayor, 'to Macimanito and all its residents. May the city and its people continue to live long and prosper for many decades to come!'

'Macimanito!' Everyone lifted their glasses to their lips and took a sip.

It was seven days since the storm. The city had returned more or less to normal, despite the damage sustained by buildings and trees. Twenty-four hours after Reggie had assured him that storms of such magnitude were a thing of the past, Mayor Klimpton had broadcast that it was safe for residents to return. At first, they trickled back in ones and twos. Then a steady stream of cars entered the city from the south. A long thread of humanity winding itself back home.

People were shocked to see the streets littered with broken branches, cladding from buildings and broken billboards. To look up and see the myriad of shattered windows in the office blocks near their homes. But within days, a community spirit had taken hold. Residents brushed debris off the pavements and put it in big wheelie bins supplied by the Council for the clean-up operation. There were only a few traces of the deluge which had swamped the city that day. The storm drains had largely done their work, leaving only a puddle here and there.

A huge, collective sigh of relief washed over the city when the Mayor appeared on local television stations to announce that violent weather fronts would not be troubling the city again. He announced that the university's departments of meteorology and electrical engineering had developed a new way of dissipating tornadoes that had been used to good effect on the day of the storm. His justification for telling this white lie was that residents were more likely to accept a solution from an academic establishment than from a thirteen-year-old girl.

'As you are aware,' Mayor Klimpton said, 'we had a very close call last week. If it hadn't been for the inquisitive nature and persistence of Lizzie here,' he nodded towards the far end of the table, 'we wouldn't all be standing here, celebrating the city's future. So, I would ask you all to raise your glasses once again, this time to Lizzie!'

'And Josh!' protested Lizzie, before anyone had taken another sip.

Josh looked mortified with embarrassment, his neck turning red above the stiff, white collar of his shirt.

'To Lizzie and Josh!' said the Mayor, lifting his glass in the air.

'To Lizzie and Josh!'

Everyone raised their glasses: Kitchi, Reggie and his team of technicians, Lizzie's mother and grandpa, Josh's parents and brother and most of the members of the Skyway Committee.

Lizzie and Josh weren't sure if they were supposed to toast themselves, so they stood there looking embarrassed.

The thick black tights her mother had insisted Lizzie wear with a red sleeveless dress and black cardigan, were making Lizzie itch. She moved one shiny leather shoe up and down the back of her leg.

'And finally!' said the Mayor.

Oh no, thought Lizzie. She was desperate to get out of such girly clothes and back into her combats. When her mother had told her they were invited to a special celebration at the Mayor's house, she had come up with every excuse she could think of not to go. But her mother had been insistent.

'In recognition of Lizzie's bravery and her role in saving the city,' he continued, 'I would like to present her with a small token of our appreciation.'

He walked round to where Lizzie was standing and handed her an envelope. She looked at it, and then up at her mother.

'Open it,' she said gently.

Lizzie slid her finger under the sealed flap and pulled out a ticket. 'A year's pass to The Badlands Science Park' it read. At the bottom, someone had hand-written 'Lizzie Chambers'. On the back, details of all the places in The Badlands to which the ticket gained her entry.

'Where are The Badlands, Mum?' she asked.

'They're east of here, in prairie country. You'll love it there, darling.'

'Lots of sciency things to do,' added her grandpa, 'among other things.' He gave her a sly wink.

'We'll take you next summer, I promise,' said her mum.

Lizzie's eyes lit up. 'Thank you, Mr Mayor.'

Josh nudged her with his elbow. 'Sounds like fun.'

While the adults chatted amongst themselves, Lizzie and Josh sneaked out. They sat at the bottom of the grand staircase made of polished wood, which swept upwards forming two arcs behind them.

'Wow! Look at this place,' said Lizzie. 'It's almost as fancy as Gildchrist's office, with all the posh leather sofas and shiny crystals. I wonder what happened to her.'

'Didn't you hear?' said Josh. 'My dad told me she and her heavies were arrested and charged on two counts of kidnapping. Gildchrist must have promised them a hefty sum of money to take the blame, as they were sentenced to five years' imprisonment and she was given only two years for conspiracy to kidnap.'

'I didn't like her,' said Lizzie. 'All she seemed to care about was getting rich. I'm glad we won't be seeing the likes of her again.'

'I'll drink to that!' said Josh, clinking his glass against Lizzie's.

ACKNOWLEDGEMENTS

'The Storm Magnet' is Book 1 of the Skyway Series, a trilogy inspired by my two-year stay in Calgary, Canada from 2015 to 2017. During two long, bitterly cold winters, I came to appreciate the +15 Skywalk – the Skyway of my book - one of the world's most extensive elevated pedestrian walkways, connecting dozens of buildings in downtown Calgary. I also fell in love with the sculpted landscape and dinosaur fossils of the Alberta Badlands, where Book 2 in the Series is set, and the fabulous Rocky Mountains, which provide the setting for Book 3. When I wasn't writing, I volunteered in 'Books Between Friends', a wonderful second-hand, not-for-profit bookshop run by Louise Nesterenko, whose energy knows no bounds. Working there gave me access to all manner of books including many written by and about Canada's indigenous people, from which I have drawn in shaping my character, Lizzie Chambers' heritage. Thank you, Louise, for putting up with me reading books when I should have been sorting and stacking them. Thanks also to TC, a fellow writer, with whom I shared my Thursdays – walking, cycling and talking books.

ABOUT THE AUTHOR

Karen I Sage qualified as an electrical engineer and worked as a journalist and editor on trade magazines. She has a fascination with science and humankind's ingenuity, a love of the natural world, and a curiosity about the supernatural, which she hopes to share with children through her works of fiction.

Printed in Poland
by Amazon Fulfillment
Poland Sp. z o.o., Wrocław

64624449R00105